P9-DXT-051

Evandro was looking at Jenna, holding out his hand to her.

Saying nothing now, only waiting for her to accept. She lifted her face, looking up at him. His strong features were shadowed in the night, and she caught the faint scent of his aftershave.

His outstretched hand touched her hair.

"Always wear it long, and loose, and lovely. It's a crime to hide it with pins."

There was a smile in his voice as he spoke, but something more than a smile. Something that seemed to reach into her, touching her deep within. With the lightest touch, his hand smoothed down the length of her hair. The sensation was so light it was scarcely there, yet it made her tremble. She could not move, not a muscle. Could only stand, gazing up at him. Eyes wide, so wide, drinking him in...wanting nothing more in all the world but to be here, like this.

Looking as she did now, for him, for this man.

For the man who was like none other in all the world. The man who of all the men in all the world had the power to make her feel as she felt now.

Dear Reader,

When my editor asked if I'd like to put a contemporary romance spin on one of the great classic novels of English literature—Charlotte Brontë's immortal *Jane Eyre*—I was torn between eagerness and terror at "meddling with a masterpiece." But the former prevailed, and the result is *Cinderella in the Boss's Palazzo*. I only hope that my attempt is seen as homage, not insult!

Although updated to the current time, and with Yorkshire-set Thornfield Hall transformed into an elegant Italian palazzo, the heart of the story remains. A young woman of courage and conviction, whom life has not treated kindly, seeks to find happiness with a man cruelly blighted by the mistakes of his youth.

I hope that both those who know and love the original will find a wry enjoyment in this adaptation, and, perhaps, that those who have not yet read Brontë's masterpiece will be enthused to do so. Mr. Rochester stole my heart when I was even younger than the original Jane Eyre, and he holds a place there to this day. Perhaps he does with you, as well...

Julia

Julia James

—

CINDERELLA IN THE BOSS'S PALAZZO

HARLEQUIN
PRESENTS

If you purchased this book without a cover you should be aware
that this book is stolen property. It was reported as "unsold and
destroyed" to the publisher, and neither the author nor the
publisher has received any payment for this "stripped book."

HARLEQUIN®
PRESENTS®

Recycling programs
for this product may
not exist in your area.

ISBN-13: 978-1-335-40399-5

Cinderella in the Boss's Palazzo

Copyright © 2021 by Julia James

All rights reserved. No part of this book may be used or reproduced in
any manner whatsoever without written permission except in the case of
brief quotations embodied in critical articles and reviews.

This is a work of fiction. Names, characters, places and incidents
are either the product of the author's imagination or are used fictitiously.
Any resemblance to actual persons, living or dead, businesses,
companies, events or locales is entirely coincidental.

This edition published by arrangement with Harlequin Books S.A.

For questions and comments about the quality of this book,
please contact us at CustomerService@Harlequin.com.

Harlequin Enterprises ULC
22 Adelaide St. West, 40th Floor
Toronto, Ontario M5H 4E3, Canada
www.Harlequin.com

Printed in U.S.A.

Julia James lives in England and adores the peaceful verdant countryside and the wild shores of Cornwall. She also loves the Mediterranean—so rich in myth and history, with its sunbaked landscapes and olive groves, ancient ruins and azure seas. "The perfect setting for romance!" she says. "Rivaled only by the lush tropical heat of the Caribbean—palms swaying by a silver-sand beach lapped by turquoise waters... What more could lovers want?"

Books by Julia James

Harlequin Presents

Billionaire's Mediterranean Proposal
Irresistible Bargain with the Greek
The Greek's Duty-Bound Royal Bride
The Greek's Penniless Cinderella

Mistress to Wife

Claiming His Scandalous Love-Child
Carrying His Scandalous Heir

One Night With Consequences

Heiress's Pregnancy Scandal

Visit the Author Profile page
at Harlequin.com for more titles.

For CB—for her immortal original

CHAPTER ONE

JENNA STARED AGAIN at the letter she was holding in her hand. Typed on thick, expensive paper, it was signed by someone calling themselves the Executive Assistant to Signor Evandro Rocceforte at Rocceforte Industriale SpA in Turin. She reread it, feeling a mixture of trepidation and gratification at the offer within.

She'd felt the same conflicting emotions the day she'd received her confirmed offer of a university place to read Modern Languages eight years ago—the offer that had dispelled all the dismissive disparagement and indifference she'd grown up with. Her degree had been proof that she was right to believe in herself, as had the teaching certificate she'd achieved after that. There was also the fact that she had survived the last four relentless years at an overlarge, understaffed primary school in one of the most deprived parts of London.

She was ready for a change, and this post, if she took it, could not be more different: tutor to a seven-year-old girl—her sole charge—working and living in a *palazzo* in Italy.

Anticipation unfurled inside her, along with a desire to accept this next challenge in her life, this complete change of scene. She wasn't outgoing or charismatic, and certainly no great beauty. She knew and had accepted that she was the kind of person who could walk into a room and no one would notice. But that wouldn't matter in her new post any more than it had mattered at the school she'd taught at.

Resolutely, she sat down at her keyboard and began to type her letter of acceptance.

Evandro Rocceforte stared darkly at his computer screen, his strong, commanding features stark, his formidably astute business mind not on the impressive company accounts displayed in front of him, but on the most recent conversation he'd had with his lawyer, who was deploring the punitive settlement he'd agreed to make his ex-wife.

In the bitter, gruellingly protracted divorce proceedings Berenice had played ruthless hardball for one purpose only. To punish him. Not just for daring to divorce her, but for a crime even greater.

For seeing through her.

For seeing through the glamour, beauty and glittering charisma she presented to the world—had once presented to him, until, disillusioned and hardened, not least by her constant infidelities, he'd seen her for the woman she truly was. Self-obsessed, manipulative, and narcissistic. A woman who lived by the motto Me, Me, Me.

She wanted every man in the world to adore her, pander to her, do what she wanted. Once, he had been such a man. Such a fool.

But no longer—regardless of Berenice's attempts to use her seductive charms to lure him back. He knew she would eventually turn on him with a savage fury when he refused to be beguiled. The way she had turned every weapon she could on him when he had finally pressed for divorce.

Including the most powerful of all.

The bleak expression that Evandro knew marred his slate-dark eyes hardened. Ever since Berenice had given birth to Amelie she'd used the child as a weapon against him, and now she had forced Evandro into a hellish, no-holds-barred custody battle.

But Evandro had fought back hard—for this was a battle he must win. He *must* protect Amelie from her toxic mother, who could no more love her own daughter than she could love any human being who was not herself. It had cost him a fortune, on top of the divorce settlement, but Berenice had eventually agreed to relinquish Amelie to him, with one further condition...

He slewed his mind away, refusing to think about the final condition Berenice had imposed on him in exchange for custody of Amelie—the vengeful threat she'd made in order to gratify her monstrous ego and assuage her fury at his rejection. But her threat would never find meat to feed on. He would make sure of it.

Since his divorce had finally come through he had celebrated his hard-won freedom up to the hilt—his torrid affair last winter with the voluptuously sultry Bianca Ingrani was proof of that. Bianca—or any of her equally attentive sisterhood—would have been only too happy to become the next Signora Rocceforte. And why not? He'd just become one of Italy's most eligible single men—mega-rich, midthirties, and with the kind of striking, powerful looks that had always drawn female eyes to him.

But affairs were all that Bianca would get—or any woman he might take into his life now.

His lawyer's objection to the final price Berenice had extracted from him sounded in his head again, but he pushed it ruthlessly aside. It would never matter—he would not permit it.

He shifted position, flexing his broad shoulders. All he'd sought with Bianca was celebration, diversion, hedonistic indulgence—only that. He took an incisive breath. He had another focus to his life now. Something far more important. Some*one* far more important.

Amelie. The child he'd fought for so relentlessly, so determinedly.

His mood grew dark again. What did he really know about fatherhood? Berenice had deliberately kept Amelie abroad with her, minimising his contact with his daughter, right up to the moment of finally conceding custody.

Well, he would do his best by Amelie, however much of a stranger he was to her. His daughter was safely here in Italy, installed in the tranquil *palazzo* that would now be her home, and her future looked good.

That was all that mattered.

'Finish all the sums, and then it will be time for lunch,' Jenna said, brightly but firmly, to her pupil.

She spoke in English for lessons, as she'd been asked to do at her appointment, but in French or Italian otherwise. Her charge, thanks to her parentage and upbringing, was trilingual, and Jenna knew it was her own ability in all three languages, as well as her experience as a primary school teacher, that had landed her this job.

Not that her young pupil was very keen on schoolwork. Getting Amelie to focus on anything, least of all maths, was a challenge. But that was not surprising.

Only very recently brought to Italy, to live with a newly divorced father she'd seen very little of up until now, the poor mite had been dragged around Europe and America all her life by her jet-setting socialite mother, living in luxury hotel suites or staying as fleeting house guests in mansions and villas from Beverly Hills to the Hamptons and back to the South of France, constantly on the move, never knowing stability or a traditional home life.

Jenna had gathered that the young girl was treated, at best, as some kind of dressed-up doll, to be shown off to cooing friends. When not useful, she had been indifferently handed back to an endless succession of nannies and maids, often for days and weeks at a time, while her mother swanned off elsewhere. Inevitably, Amelie's education had suffered, and Jenna had been tasked with trying to bring her up to speed, preparing her to start school in the autumn.

Jenna's eyes went to the sash windows of the spacious room that had been set aside as a schoolroom, glancing out over the gardens beyond, verdant in the early summer sunshine. It must surely help that the little girl now finally had a chance of a stable home life here at this beautiful *palazzo*, set deep in the Italian countryside amongst rolling hills, farmland and vineyards, with wonderful gardens and extensive grounds to play in, an outdoor swimming pool to enjoy, and woods beyond to explore.

Jenna had been enchanted by the eighteenth-century *palazzo* from the moment of her arrival three weeks ago. A miniature masterpiece, built as a rural retreat for a now extinct aristocratic family, it was beautifully decorated, with painted ceilings and walls stencilled with classical-style murals. The wide sash windows were draped in light-coloured, delicately patterned silk curtains, and the elegant fireplaces were all gleaming white marble, like the floors. It couldn't have been more different from the ugly concrete-block urban school she'd taught at in London.

How incredibly lucky I was to get this job, she

thought appreciatively. *And as it's only till the autumn, I'll make sure to make the very most of it.*

Her thoughts were recalled to her charge, whose fair head was now bent—brow furrowed in novel concentration—over her work. Jenna found herself wondering just who the little girl took after. She had seen a photograph of Amelie's mother, set on the little girl's dressing table—looking glamorous, as any self-respecting jet-setting socialite should—but apart from the shape of her face and her brown eyes, there seemed little resemblance. Amelie's mother was dark-haired—so had the little girl's blond locks come from her father's side?

From what Jenna had learned from the house-keeper, Signora Farrafacci, an English woman who had married an Italian, Amelie's father was from a prestigious Northern Italian family which had come to wealth and prominence in the nineteenth century, when Italy had started to industrialise.

'Will Amelie's father be living here too?' Jenna had asked, as there had been no sign of him when she'd arrived, nor since. Other than her young charge she had only seen the staff who looked after the *palazzo*, and she found herself hoping that Amelie had not simply been shuffled from one absent parent to another.

She knew from experience that it was all too easy for the children of divorced parents to slip between the cracks—to be important to no one, and parked wherever might be the least inconvenient for the parents. Made invisible.

As I was...

She did not want that to be Amelie's fate.

'Signor Rocceforte likes to visit whenever he can, but he is a very busy man—one of Italy's top industrialists!' the housekeeper had answered Jenna proudly. 'So his arrival is never predictable. I keep everything in good order, and it would be prudent for you—' she'd cast an eye at Jenna '—to bear in mind that he may arrive at any point. He is a good employer,' she went on meaningfully, 'but he does not suffer fools gladly. He'll want to see what progress the little *signorina* is making.'

As she checked Amelie's work now, Jenna hoped he would appreciate that maths was not proving to be his daughter's best subject...

'The more you do, the easier they'll be,' she said encouragingly.

'But I don't *like* it!' Amelie retorted. 'Maman never does *anything* she doesn't like. She gets angry if someone tries to make her. She throws things! She threw a shoe at a maid once, because she brought her the wrong colour scarf. The heel was sharp and it made the maid's cheek bleed. She ran out and that made Maman angrier, yelling at her to come back. Then she sent me out of her bedroom, because she said I made things worse...'

The speech, which had started with an air of defiance, ended with a quiet trailing off. There was a pinched, unhappy look on the girl's face, and Jenna found her heart squeezing with both pity...and memory. Memory of her father's wife snapping at her to get out of the way, to stop making a nuisance of herself...

To divert Amelie from her distressing thoughts, Jenna chose her words carefully. 'Do you know, there's a saying in England that goes, *Keep your temper; nobody wants it*?' she said lightly.

For a moment, the unhappy, pinched look was still on the little girl's face, and then, to Jenna's relief, she broke into a smile.

'That's funny!' she exclaimed. '*Keep your temper; nobody wants it!*' she repeated in a sing-song voice. Then her expression changed again. 'Do you think my *papà* will lose his temper with me?' she asked, and the fearful, unhappy look was back on her face.

'I'm sure he won't,' Jenna said.

After an ill-tempered and capricious mother, the last thing Amelie needed was a critical father finding fault with her.

She needs love, and warmth, and open affection—and to know above all that she is wanted and valued. Something I didn't ever know...

Setting aside Amelie's schoolwork, they went down to lunch and did what they always did when the weather was fine—took their food outside to eat on the wide, paved terrace overlooking the spacious gardens.

Jenna looked with growing fondness at her charge as the little girl tucked into an appetising chicken salad.

I see so much of myself in her—uprooted, anxious

and unsure. Wanted by no one. Doomed to a lonely childhood... I don't want that for Amelie.

But that depended on the little girl's still absent father.

Would he come home soon? No one seemed to know.

Evandro glanced out of the window, impatient to land and deplane. His non-stop schedule had taken him across Europe and up and down Italy, checking on various multimillion-euro projects and assessing and clinching potential new ventures first-hand.

He had crammed three months of business travel into three weeks for one purpose only—to clear his diary and enable him to get to the *palazzo.* To see the little girl he had finally extracted from the unloving arms of her vengeful mother. To give her a better life.

I'll build a good relationship with her—even though I'll have to learn from scratch. I'll protect her from the ills of her mother—protect her always... whatever it takes.

Like a sudden shadow over the bright sun, his lawyer's warning sounded in his head.

'Do you realise the implications?' his lawyer had asked forebodingly.

Evandro had looked the man in the eye. 'They won't apply,' he'd answered tersely. Then, with a twist of his mouth, he'd added, 'Not after finally escaping ten years of a hellish marriage. No, it's

Amelie who is the focus of my attention now—she's my only priority.'

A priority he would be making real from this very day onward.

The plane's wheels touched down with the merest bump, and minutes later he was on his way to his office. He had a few essential debriefings to get through before he could go to his apartment and pack for the *palazzo*. Then he would take the autostrada south. To Amelie.

Jenna glanced up at the sky, still overcast from the rain earlier that day. Dusk was gathering, but this was her first chance of fresh air today and she wasn't going to miss it. Amelie had opted for staying indoors with the housekeeper, playing noisy card games with her and the two maids, Maria and Loretta.

Jenna would be back in time for the little girl's supper, but for now she was enjoying her walk along the woodland path that emerged at the top of the private road to the *palazzo*, which wound steeply uphill from the public highway a kilometre below. Lower down, another path would allow her to cut back up to the grand front entrance of the *palazzo*.

On her way down, the narrow road kinked around a rocky outcrop, and she gave a little gasp to see there had been a rockfall; heavy scree and large boulders littered the road's surface. She surmised that it had been caused by the heavy rain they'd had, loosening the soil on the side of the hill.

The spread was extensive, and as she stared she saw it was potentially dangerous. Any vehicle approaching from the highway, slewing as it must around the outcrop, would not see the rockfall until it was upon it. This would put it at risk of hitting it full on, or swerving towards the sheer drop to the valley on the other side.

As she hovered, wondering what she should do, knowing she needed to get back to the *palazzo* to alert the staff of what had happened, she froze. She could distinctly hear the noise of a car, turning off the public highway and roaring uphill with a throaty growl of acceleration. In moments it would reach the outcrop, swerve around it…and hit the littered boulders.

She ran forward, scrambling over the fallen boulders and rounding the outcrop. The daylight was fast fading and the oncoming vehicle had its headlights blazing, pinioning her in their glare in the middle of the road, right in the car's speeding path. For a second terror seized her, and then, with a screech of tyres, the car—some low-slung, flashy-looking monster of a car—ground to a halt.

The engine cut out but Jenna couldn't move, fear pinning her in place. Then someone was getting out, slamming the driver's door angrily.

As angrily as he snarled words in a burst of furious Italian. '*Idiota!* What the hell do you think you're doing, running into the middle of the road? I could have killed you!'

He stood, silhouetted in the glare of his car's

headlights, towering over her, his strongly planed face cast into stark relief by the glaring headlights. His charcoal business suit sheathed broad shoulders and long legs, its superb cut—along with the grey silk tie and gold tic pin— telling her just as clearly as the obviously expensive car that there was only one person this scathingly irate man could possibly be.

This was Evandro Rocccforte.

CHAPTER TWO

JENNA FELT HER heart sink—then she rallied again. Her chin went up.

'*Mi dispiace.*' Her voice was breathless and shaky, but she ploughed on. 'I had to stop you!' She reverted to English, not knowing the Italian translation for what she had to explain. 'There's been a rockfall just around the outcrop.'

She gestured sweepingly with her hand and saw her employer frown. Without a word he strode past her, to see for himself. Then he turned.

The furious look had gone from his face, but it remained dark.

Impressions tumbled through Jenna's mind—irrelevant to the moment but pushing into her consciousness all the same. Her overpowering initial impression of a man with formidable presence had lessened not one iota. Nor had the visceral impact of his height and powerful body.

'That's a hell of a mess,' he said, his face tightening in angry displeasure.

He frowned, looking back at his car and then

striding to it to turn off the headlights. Then he got out his phone, speaking into it rapidly in curt Italian, too fast for Jenna to follow. Hanging up, he slid the phone back in his inner jacket pocket and looked across at her again.

He frowned, as if seeing her for the first time. 'So, just who are you?' he demanded. Realisation clearly sinking in, he answered his own question. 'Ah, of course—the English teacher.' He gave a short, sardonic laugh. 'You look more like some kind of woodland sprite, melding into the landscape at dusk. Well—' his voice became brisk '—get yourself back to the *palazzo*. Take care as you go. They're coming down to collect me, and to block the entrance to the drive so no one else risks their lives here. They'll clear the rockfall in the morning.'

He turned away, striding back to his car, and Jenna watched him yank open the boot, extracting some luggage. Then, mindful of his order—for an order it certainly had been—she retraced her steps around the outcrop, picking her way carefully through the rockfall to gain the path back up through the woods.

Her thoughts were hectic.

So, that's Amelie's father.

She lifted aside the drooping branch of a tree, quickening her pace. He'd yelled at her and given orders, and he looked every inch a rich, powerful captain of industry and the owner of a historic *palazzo*. But there had been something else in his tone... She heard it in her mind again—the short, sardonic humour in his voice as he'd likened her to a wood-land sprite.

That, surely, was out of character?

But it was not her ponderings over his character that dominated her thoughts as she emerged into the extensive rear gardens at the *palazzo*. It was that for-midable impression of height, a powerful physique, strong, arresting features and a deep, mesmerising voice that burned in her consciousness.

She felt her heart rate quicken with her pace, and hurried on.

When she got inside, it was to find the *palazzo* humming like a disturbed beehive, thanks to the unscheduled arrival of its owner. The staff were bustling about and Signora Farrafacci only briefly paused to inform her that Amelie was to dine with her father, and that Jenna's own dinner would be brought up to her quarters later.

Jenna retreated gratefully, taking refuge in the large, generously appointed bedroom and adjoin-ing sitting room she had been allocated on one of the upper floors of the *palazzo*. A connecting door linked her sitting room to a mirror room on the other side, set up as Amelie's playroom, which the little girl's own bedroom opened off.

She crossed now to the window in her sitting room, sliding it up and leaning on the sill with her elbows, breathing in the soft mild air, scented with the honeysuckle growing far below. Night had gath-ered completely now, and she could hear owls hoot-ing mournfully in the woods beyond the gardens.

Her abrupt, adrenaline-fuelled encounter with her charge's father replayed in her mind with vivid impact—and not just because of the danger she had both invited and averted by impulsively running forward to warn him of the hidden rockfall. His tall, powerful, broad-chested physique and frowning brows were also vivid in her mind's eye. As was the way he had yelled at her angrily for running into the path of his car.

Her chin lifted defiantly.

Well, if I hadn't, both he and his horribly expensive car might now be at the foot of the valley, smashed to pieces!

She walked through into her bedroom, and on impulse decided to have a leisurely bath while waiting for her dinner to arrive. Baths were a rare and luxurious indulgence for her; showers were quicker and more efficient.

As she sank into the deep waters she found herself replaying, yet again, that encounter with her employer. But not, this time, his initial harsh words to her. Rather, that throwaway likening of her to a woodland sprite...

It was a description of her that was as fanciful as it was unlikely. Sprites were elfin and beautiful—they were always described as beautiful. She was nothing like that.

She was of medium height, with medium-length hair—always neatly confined in a French plait. Slightly built, she wore clothes chosen for practicality and comfort. Her unremarkable looks were the opposite of eye-catching, and she did not bother with make-up—it was not needed in the classroom, and her limited social life was mostly confined to school functions with her colleagues.

So, no—nothing like a woodland dryad. Nothing at all. What on earth had made him say such a thing?

As she slid deeper into the warm water she felt it lapping her body like a caress. Around her shoulders her loosened hair floated freely, and the water buoyed her whole body, almost to make her float. It felt warm and sensuous, playing at the sensitive points of her wrists as her hands hovered in the water.

A strangely dreamy mood started to overcome her, induced by the heat of the water, the steamy atmosphere of the thickened air she was breathing and the feeling of absolute relaxation as she gave herself to the moment. The single soft light above the vanity unit added to her languor, bestowing upon her an awareness of her physical body, the weightlessness of it in the shimmering water.

She let her eyes fall shut, lids lowering into drowsy somnolence, yet she was still conscious of the contours of her half-floating naked body… In the darkness behind her closed eyelids an image of her employer sprang to life, strong and vivid—as if he were beholding her vulnerable nakedness as she lay there, his dark gaze sweeping over her, enjoying what he saw…

She surfaced with a start, her eyes flying open as she levered herself upward, her soaking wet hair instantly heavy and soggy on her shoulders and back. Her cheeks heated suddenly—and not from the heat of the bathwater. She shook her head, as if to shake that thought, wherever it had come from—however it had come to her—right out of her brain, where it had no business to be.

She took a breath, staring at the tiled wall at the foot of the capacious bathtub, blinking to dissipate the vivid—and unbidden—image. Then, resolutely, she reached for the bar of soap and the bottle of shampoo to get on with the actual point of bathing—to get herself clean.

And not—*not*—to indulge in thoughts that were as inexplicable as they were outrageous.

With vigorous movements she soaped herself briskly, shampooed her hair, then set the bath to drain and turned the shower head on as cold as she could bear it to rinse off not just the soap and shampoo but her outrageous thoughts as well.

Ten minutes later, wrapped in her sensible dressing gown and wearing her sensible cotton pyjamas, she was sitting on the sofa in front of the TV, switching on the English news channel. After dinner she'd check her lesson plans for the next morning and jot down a brief report on Amelie's progress so far, in case her employer enquired about it.

Her *employer*.

She repeated the word firmly to herself.

The tap on her door announcing the arrival of her dinner was timely.

* * *

Evandro stood out on the terrace overlooking the gardens, hands thrust into his trouser pockets, looking out into the night. High in the sky, the moon appeared to be moving through the scudding clouds. An illusion, just like so much in life was.

Like his bride had been.

He frowned. Why the hell was he thinking of his wedding day, ten long, damnable years ago? A day that, for all the vast sums of money spent on it, had been a sham. Their lavish, no-expenses-spared wedding had been like Evandro's bride—as gaudy as a carnival float and just as shoddy...fake and cheating.

Berenice—seductively sensual, dripping in diamonds, her wedding dress having cost as much as a house—had revelled in being the glittering star of the whole over-the-top show, and it had been splashed all over the gushing celebrity magazines with himself cast as the adoring bridegroom, dazzled by her brilliance and beauty.

His frown deepened. How, just *how* had he come to be so incomprehensibly stupid?

His jaw tensed. He knew exactly how he'd become that stupid, that gullible.

He had been led by the nose by the woman he'd married...and urged on by his father.

He could hear the older man's eager words even now.

'She's got everything...absolutely everything. Ravishingly beautiful, and with her father dead now

she inherits all the voting stock in Trans-Montane that we need.'

It had seemed a combination made in heaven.

It had turned out to have originated in hell instead.

But out of it had come Amelie.

His expression changed. The meeting between them this evening had been strained—she'd been shy and subdued, the same way she had been when he'd collected her at the airport on her arrival from Paris, bringing her here to the *palazzo* three weeks ago. But that would change, given time. Time he would devote to her.

As for the woman he'd hired to be Amelie's teacher... He frowned now, as he tried to remember her unremarkable features... She would simply have to work around the time he spent with her pupil.

He frowned again, shifting position once more. The woman had rushed headlong into the path of his speeding car, as if discounting the possibility of her own destruction in order to warn him of the possibility of his. His expression flickered. Had her behaviour been recklessness...or courage?

Or both?

Jenna walked down the wide marble staircase to the grand entrance hall, carrying Amelie's schoolbooks and artwork. The expected summons to report on her pupil's progress had come, and now she knocked lightly on the door of the library before entering.

She'd left Amelie up in the schoolroom with a

spelling worksheet to get on with. The little girl's mood this morning, following her father's arrival the evening before, was… Jenna sought for the right word before settling on *unsure*.

She could understand it well enough. She, too, felt a flutter of trepidation now, as she walked into the large, book-lined room, with its imposing fireplace flanked by deep leather armchairs.

Illuminated by large French doors—open to the terrace today, to admit fresh air—was a desk of considerable size and grandeur, bearing a PC and some paperwork. Seated behind it was her employer.

Jenna deliberately used the word inside her head, to counter the sudden tightening of her stomach muscles as he looked up. The impact he made on her was just as instant, just as powerful, as it had been last night. That impression of toughness and power was every bit as overwhelming.

But she must not let herself be overwhelmed. She was being summoned to give an account of her progress—or not—with Amelie, and the man she was approaching would likely make an impact on anyone approaching for any reason at all.

He had a presence about him, Jenna found herself thinking. A look of formidable gravitas which presumably went with being the head of an international company with global reach, turning over huge revenues and employing vast numbers. There was no doubt he was a man of power and responsibility.

Currently, he was observing her approach with

an unreadable expression, deep lines carved around his mouth.

What's caused those deep lines? What has he had to endure?

The questions flitted across the surface of Jenna's mind, unbidden.

She pressed her mouth tightly. It was irrelevant—absolutely irrelevant—what he looked like, or what experiences in life he'd been through. Just as the impact of his powerful physique, strongly saturnine looks and air of wealth and gravitas was nothing to her.

She stopped in front of the desk as he gave her a curt nod and bade her to sit on the chair set for her.

'So, Miss Ayrton...' he addressed her in English, his deep voice brisk and only slightly accented. 'How have things been with Amelie these first few weeks? Please make your account as brief as possible.'

Jenna placed the bundle of paperwork she had brought down with her carefully on the desk, away from his own papers, and calmly and concisely ran through her assessment of Amelie's current educational level, before moving on to where she was focusing her efforts—on building key skills in reading, comprehension and maths, plus providing a general syllabus of geography, history and basic science.

She was in mid flow, pointing out the developmental impact of Amelie being multilingual, when her employer raised a hand to silence her.

'Enough,' he said curtly. 'Show me her exercise books.'

He held out a hand in a peremptory fashion, and Jenna docilely handed him the required items. He flicked through them, then handed them back, making no comment.

'Amelie *is* making progress.' Jenna wanted him to know that. 'Having lacked formal schooling, her biggest educational challenge is application,' she went on. 'Of course, that is true for children generally—play is nearly always preferred to work!'

A sardonic expression formed on her employer's face. 'And not only by children, Miss Ayrton,' he observed caustically.

Jenna looked at him, uncertain as to whether to smile. He might have intended that as a humorous remark, but it was impossible to discern. So she simply nodded, and then continued, picking her words with care.

'Routine and stability,' she said, 'are essential for children—especially to develop focus, concentration and attention span. I acknowledge the fact that has been largely absent up till now.'

She saw her employer's face darken sharply.

'She's been dragged from pillar to post across Europe and the USA all her life. It's a wonder the child can read, let alone anything else.'

The harshness in his voice echoed the tone he'd used the night before, when he'd excoriated her for running into the path of his car.

Jenna said nothing. It was not her place to comment on the friction that she knew, after many all-too-often fraught parent-teacher evenings, could erupt between warring divorced parents.

Then, abruptly, the anger was gone. And in a voice that was not harsh, merely brisk, he addressed her again.

'Is there anything she *is* good at?' he demanded.

Jenna did not trouble to hide the shocked look on her face. 'Yes, of course!' she retorted roundly. 'Maths may never prove to be Amelie's strong suit,' she allowed, 'but art and creativity definitely will be.'

She extracted several sheets of art paper, showing the top one to Evandro.

'Look how good this is! Oh, not necessarily in terms of technical execution—that will come in time—but in imagination and use of colour. And this one too.' She slid out the next one to hold it up. 'And this—'

She let her employer's dark-eyed gaze peruse—impassively—the fruits of his daughter's artistic labour, which depicted a mix of multitowered fairy-tale castles, populated by fantastical animals and opulently dressed princesses.

'Any and all ability and enthusiasm should always be encouraged and fostered,' she went on resolutely, suddenly urgently wanting to defend Amelie from her father's potential criticism. Wanting him not to be critical at all.

Jenna's chin went up, and she looked straight at him. She refused to be cowed by his forbidding

expression, and was determined to have her say…
to make him see. This was for Amelie, a little girl
whose father should praise her and value her.

As mine never did.

Remembered pain bit at her. She did not want
that for Amelie.

'It's vital—*essential*—for children to be encouraged,
to know there is something they have a flair for. No
child should *ever* be made to feel worthless or useless.'

There was a passion and a vehemence in her voice
she could not hide as memories scythed through her
mind. Bad memories—of her father's dismissive
criticism, his impatient indifference…

She became aware that she was under perusal.
Not the employer-employee kind of perusal, to discover whether she was adequately performing the
job for which she had been hired; there was something different in his assessment of her.

Then it was gone.

He sat back in his chair—a large, modern, leather,
executive-style chair, at odds with the antique desk
and leather-bound gold trimmed books lining all the
walls. Making no comment on what she'd urged, he
simply said, with a brief nod, 'Very well—thank you
for your report. Continue with what you are doing.
That said…' his gaze flicked over her '…you must be
prepared to rearrange lessons on the fly and without
notice. They are not a priority while I am here. My
time with Amelie is the priority. Now, have you any
questions of me? If not, then go back to your pupil.'

Jenna got to her feet, gathering up Amelie's

schoolwork. She wanted to get one more vital message across, to fight Amelie's corner for her.

'Though it isn't my place to say so, Signor Rocceforte, I completely agree that lessons aren't a priority for Amelie right now. It's far better, with your having been away for so long, that she has extensive quality time with you—'

'You are quite right, Miss Ayrton,' he cut across her, his voice brusque, his expression closed. 'It isn't your place to say so.'

For a second she froze, feeling the force of his displeasure at her intrusive comment just as she'd felt the force of his fury last night. But just as she had last night, she rallied. What she'd said had been for her charge's sake—for the sake of a little girl who reminded her so much of herself, wrenched from all she knew to be abruptly taken to live with her father, a stranger to her.

Please let it be better for Amelie than it was for me. Let her father want to bond with her, spend time with her, become a good, loving father to her.

The silent plea was strong and heartfelt.

She looked across at Evandro. His expression was forbidding, but for Amelie's sake she had to get through to him—make him see how vital it was for his daughter that, however much of a stranger he was to her, he must reach out to her. She would not shy away from telling him so.

She stood in front of him, her shoulders squared. 'My place, Signor Rocceforte, as Amelie's teacher, is to look out for the best interests of my pupil,' she said, quietly but unflinchingly, unapologetically, her eyes steadily on him.

He was a man of power and wealth, but to her, right now, he was merely her charge's father—the man who had a responsibility for his daughter's emotional well-being, a responsibility not to blight her childhood any more than it already had been.

'My responsibility,' she went on, never taking her eyes from him, 'is only and always to Amelie. She is a fractured child, a child from a broken home and, however affluent her upbringing has been, it has lacked what she needs most—stability, constancy and security. The security not just of routine and pre-dictability, but also, far more essentially, the secu-rity of knowing she is valued, wanted…and loved.' A low, compelling insistence filled her voice now, and her gaze was resolute on Evandro. 'That last above all.'

She turned away, not caring what his reaction might be, and walked to the door and opened it, leaving the room and the formidable Italian behind.

As the door closed, shutting her away from sight, Evandro looked at the place where she had been. His expression flickered. If he'd had to go into a witness box to give evidence of the clothes she'd been wear-ing, what height she was, what her eye colour was, he'd have no idea at all.

Yet he could have repeated, word for word, what she'd just said to him in her quiet, pointed address. *'Valued, wanted…and loved.'*

The triad echoed in his mind. Well, the first, surely, he could testify to—the grim face of his lawyer as he'd perused the sum his client had been prepared to hand over to Amelie's mother was proof of that. And the second he could also testify to—as evidenced by the bitter year-long custody war.

But the third...?

He felt himself shying away from the word, remembering instead the deliberately cruel words hurled at him by his jibing wife.

Abruptly, he pushed back his chair, getting to his feet, walking to the French doors and pushing them open. He suddenly needed fresh air.

CHAPTER THREE

JENNA AND AMELIE were left to lunch on their own, but it was served in the schoolroom, not out on the terrace where, presumably, they might have disturbed her father at work in the library.

Amelie's mood was still unsettled, and Jenna decided diversion was needed. She could do with diversion herself, as her final words to Evandro that morning were still echoing in her mind. Had he taken offence, been angered by them? She did not care if he had—only if he chose to ignore them. For she stood by every single word she'd said to him.

'We'll go on a nature walk!' she announced, and Amelie's little face brightened.

They went out to the terrace, ready to set off across the extensive gardens.

'Where I taught in London,' Jenna said, 'there were no fields, no woods—so think how lucky you are to have all this beautiful countryside and these beautiful gardens,' she said, gesturing expansively with her arms at their surroundings as they headed off.

A voice behind her spoke. 'I'm glad you think so.'

She turned, surprised and taken aback. Evandro was approaching them, rapidly closing in on them with his long strides.

'I saw you through the library window. Where are you off to?' he asked.

Aware of Amelie slipping her little hand into hers, as if for reassurance, Jenna said, as composedly as she could, 'A nature walk through the gardens.'

'May I come with you?'

Jenna looked at him in surprise. Not just because of what he'd asked. But because his tone of voice was so different from the brusqueness of her interview with him that morning. Then she realised why. It was for his daughter—not for her.

And she was glad of it. Glad to see him—the first time she'd seen him with Amelie—being so different from the forbidding way he'd been with her that morning. He was addressing his daughter directly now, still with the same genial tone of voice.

'What do you think, Amelie? I'm sure there are things about nature that Miss Jenna could teach me, as well as you. I know very little, for example, about the domestic habits of slugs.'

Was there some deadpan humour in his declaration? Jenna could not decide—just as she couldn't know whether he'd intended humour in his remark to her that morning about adults, too, preferring play to work.

She could still feel the little hand in hers, and knew that it meant Amelie felt, as she did herself, unsure about Evandro's sudden presence. A little ache formed in her. Every child needed to be wanted by their father—not to be ignored by them. Invisible to them.

Amelie was looking wary. 'I don't like slugs,' she said.

'Fortunately,' her father observed, his voice dry, 'slugs like each other. So there will be lots of baby slugs in the spring.'

'Slugs are hermaphrodites. So are snails,' Jenna heard herself saying.

The new word had caught Amelie's curiosity. 'What's that mean?' she asked.

'Every slug is both a girl and a boy,' Jenna explained. 'So they make babies with each other. It can sound odd to us, but it's natural to them.'

'I wouldn't want to be a boy as well,' Amelie declared. 'I wouldn't want to be a boy at all!'

'You're exactly right just as you are,' Evandro said decisively. 'And I'm very glad,' he went on, 'that you've come here to live with me.'

Jenna heard the warmth in his voice as he spoke to Amelie, and felt her own uncertainty ease a fraction. He was saying the right things—making his daughter feel welcome, making it clear that she belonged here in the *palazzo* with him—and that had to be good.

He gestured towards the gardens, speaking in the same good-humoured tones. 'Now, what about this nature walk—where are we off to?'

'I thought we might go into the rose garden and

watch the bees collect nectar, and find out how that helps the roses and the other flowers,' replied Jenna.

She found herself noticing what a difference it made when Evandro unbent. A welcome difference, definitely. But it was not, she reminded herself, on her account. She knew why he'd joined their little expedition, and knew her role now was to act as bridge between father and daughter. The nature walk would be an occasion for the two of them to spend time together that need not be focused entirely on each other, but on a shared activity, so they could get used to being around each other.

She led the way onwards, deliberately letting Amelie's fingers casually slip from hers as they went into the circular rose garden. The afternoon sun beat down, and Jenna hoped it would not be too hot. She and Amelie were in summery clothes, but her employer was in a business suit. Although, it was lightweight, in a superbly cut dark grey material—that matched, she thought irrelevantly, his dark, slate-grey eyes.

She led them to a beautiful dark red rose, carefully folded back its velvet petals, and started to explain pollination. 'Now let's see if we can spot any bees visiting the roses,' she ended.

'There's one,' she heard Evandro observe, pointing to another rose that a fat bee was investigating.

'So it is! And look, Amelie, you can see the yellow pollen from a previous flower on its legs.'

They watched the bee at work for a while, then it buzzed away, and Jenna led the way out of the rose garden. She was pleased to see that Amelie was beside her father now, as they took the path to the ornamental pond in the centre of the gardens. He was talking to her, still in that good-humoured, reassuring fashion, describing how these gardens had been laid out over two hundred years ago, when the *palazzo* had been built.

'One day this week,' Evandro was saying, 'we'll get the fountain in the middle of the pond working. The water comes from a spring higher up the hill, beyond the woods.'

He kept talking, explaining the rudiments of the fountain's mechanism. Just how much of the science Amelie was taking in, Jenna wasn't sure. But the important thing was that she was paying attention—and that she was with her father.

Her eyes went to the tall figure perched, like Amelie, on the stone rim of the pond. She'd avoided looking directly at him since he'd emerged to join them, but now, as he and Amelie talked together, she found her gaze stealing to him. It was extraordinary, she thought, how different he was being now that he was with his daughter. Oh, the gravitas was still there, but it was leavened…lightened. She found her gaze wanting to linger…

Then, thankfully, he was standing up. 'Shall we head back?' he suggested.

Jenna nodded, letting them take the lead, walking behind. She tried to focus on how good it was that Amelie and her father were together like this rather than on how broad his shoulders were, how sable his dark hair, how deep his voice…

As they regained the terrace, she made to lead Amelie back to the classroom, but she was halted.

'Amelie, please go and ask Signora Farrafacci for refreshments to be brought out here. You must be thirsty—I know I am. And Miss Jenna, too, no doubt.' He turned to her and raised an eyebrow in a quizzical, sardonic manner. 'Being an English-woman, you must surely think it's time for after-noon tea?'

Amelie skipped off, glad to postpone any resumption of lessons, and Jenna suddenly felt awkward, self-conscious at being left on her own with her employer like this.

But why am I being like this about him? she wondered. *He's just the father of my pupil.*

And that, surely, was no reason to feel awkward and self-conscious…

'Come and sit down,' he said, pulling out one of the chairs at a table under a wide parasol.

The shade was distinctly welcome to Jenna and she did as she was bade, hoping Amelie would return quickly.

Evandro settled himself down at the table, too, opposite her, pausing only to shrug off his jacket and hook it around the back of a spare chair, loosening his tie thereafter. The casual way in which he did it made the atmosphere informal in a way that contrasted starkly with his brusque, businesslike formality from the library that morning.

* * *

'So,' Evandro said, easing back into the padded chair, 'am I making progress, do you think? Being a good father?'

He let his eyes rest on the woman who had stood up to him without hesitation or diffidence to make it clear what fatherhood was all about.

She held her ground now, too, as she answered him.

'Yes,' she said plainly. 'Amelie became noticeably more at ease with you as our walk progressed.'

He saw her pause for a moment, and take a breath.

'She is bound to be a little shy at first, but if you draw her out, praise her, encourage her, she will blossom, I know she will.'

He heard the warmth in her voice—and something more than warmth. He frowned inwardly. It had almost been a plea.

Now, why should that be?

The musing question hung in his head for a moment, and then she was speaking again.

'I hope,' she said, more hesitantly now, 'that you don't object to the idea of my teaching Amelie outside of the schoolroom sometimes?'

He waved a hand—not to silence her, but in an expansive gesture. 'If today is an example of your approach, I'm fine with that.' He paused, then continued, 'Overall I'm fine, Miss Ayrton, with what you are doing and achieving with Amelie.'

He paused again, conscious that there was something he must say. Something he owed her.

'I apologise if I was…brusque…this morning. You must understand…' He felt a frown form on his face. 'I am new to all this.' He fastened his eyes on hers, intent on getting his next point clearly across to her. 'My absence from Amelie's life so far has not been with my consent. She has finally come here to live, however, and I shall be doing my best to give her the safe and happy childhood she deserves—the kind of childhood you so eloquently urged me to provide.'

He saw her colour slightly, noticing almost absently that it brought a discernible improvement to her pale cheeks. Out of nowhere, he found himself wishing she was wearing something less nondescript than the beige knee-length skirt and indifferently styled matching blouse which did nothing for her.

No one should be allowed to look so dowdy, he thought with passing disapproval.

Then she was speaking, and his thoughts went from her lacklustre appearance to what she was saying.

'I'm sorry if I was stating the obvious,' she replied, in a quiet, but far from diffident way, 'but you see the children of divorced parents can often become —'

She stopped abruptly, and Evandro frowned. 'Become what?' he prompted.

'Invisible,' she answered flatly.

She dropped her eyes, looking down at her hands, folded in her lap, the knuckles suddenly white.

His frown deepened. Clearly this was not just about Amelie…

'You say that,' he said slowly, his eyes not leaving her, 'as if you have experience of it yourself?'

Hazel eyes lifted suddenly to his.

No, not hazel alone. Hazel with a flash of forest green in the depths.

'Yes,' she said, in that plain way she had. But only that one word.

'Tell me more,' he commanded.

It was important, he told himself, that he understood what might be affecting Amelie.

Then he gave a quick shake of his head. 'I apologise—I do not mean to speak so brusquely. But I am used to giving orders.' His face twisted. 'I am not a man of airs and graces—I speak as I find. But for all that...' he drew breath '...please explain, if you will. For Amelie's sake.'

He saw her expression flicker, but whether it was at his words or memories of her own he could not tell. Then she was speaking again, and he could see her fingers tighten in her lap.

'Children know when they are not wanted,' she said, her voice low. 'And they learnt to...to adapt their behaviour accordingly. So—'

She broke off, and for a moment Evandro assumed she was reluctant to say more. Then he realised she had seen Amelie, as he now had, emerging from the *palazzo*, followed by one of the maids carrying a tray of refreshments.

He felt a stab of frustration that their arrival had silenced Miss Ayrton. Then, mindful of the moment, he thanked the maid as she placed the tray on the table and bade Amelie to take her seat.

There was a pot of tea for Miss Ayrton, strong coffee for himself, and a jug of fresh orange juice for Amelie, together with another of iced water for them all, and a plate of biscotti.

He watched as Miss Ayrton poured some orange juice for her pupil, diluting it heavily with water. 'Very healthy,' he observed, reaching for his coffee.

'Signorina Jenna says too many fizzy drinks make your teeth fall out,' Amelie informed him with an air of virtue as she took a gulp of her juice.

Evandro nodded. 'Quite true,' he said, straight-faced. 'I knew of someone whose teeth fell out—all of them, all at once—right in the middle of his making a speech at a grand dinner. The audience was very glad, as his speech was very boring. He's had to wear false teeth ever since—and because they don't fit properly they click when he speaks. Like this...'

He made the appropriate noise, and Amelie giggled. It felt good to hear. Of their own accord, his eyes went past the little girl to her teacher, as if seeking her approval, and he caught the slight smile on her face as she poured herself a cup of tea. He noticed how some colour had tinged her pale cheeks, and how a smile, however slight, seemed to improve her nondescript appearance.

He found himself wanting to see her smile again. And then wondered why. Jenna Ayrton was here to teach Amelie. That was all.

He turned back to her pupil. 'I am pleased to hear

that you are making progress so you can be ready for school in the autumn. How much are you learning about your new home country of Italy?' He smiled at Amelie, wanting to draw her out. Wanting to show her teacher he was making the effort to do so.

'We are doing lots of history and learning about the mountains and rivers. And where the cities are,' Amelie answered, and then reeled off the names, in English and Italian, of half a dozen.

'Very good.' Evandro nodded approvingly. 'What about the city I work in?'

'Turin,' Amelie supplied. 'Torino in Italian.'

'Esattamente!'

He went on to ask her about Italy's mountains, telling her he liked to go skiing on them in winter, and saying she might like to come too next time, after Christmas.

'Would you like that?' he asked. 'You could try skiing, or snowboarding, or just stick to tobogganing.' His gaze flicked to Miss Ayrton, sipping her tea quietly, and suddenly he wanted to draw her out as well. 'Do you enjoy winter sports, Miss Ayrton?' he asked.

She looked startled at his suddenly addressing her, but then replied in the quiet way he was becoming used to.

'I've never done any,' she answered.

Amelie turned to her teacher, her expression animated. 'You could come with us!' she said.

She shook her head. 'I'll be gone by winter, Amelie,' she replied. 'As soon as you've started school I'll be going back to England.'

Evandro saw Amelie's face fall. Unease welled in him.

Amelie must never grow close to any woman— it's too dangerous.

In his head, his lawyer's warning echoed yet again, carrying with it Berenice's final venom. He, too, must never grow close to any woman in his life…

He shook away his uneasy thoughts. That warning might be true in general, but it was utterly irrelevant to the current situation. Jenna Ayrton— a woman no man would even notice was in the room—was Amelie's temporary teacher, nothing more.

And once Amelie was settled into school she'd soon forget all about her.

And so, obviously, would he.

CHAPTER FOUR

JENNA CHECKED HER appearance in the elegant cheval glass in her bedroom. Somewhat to her surprise, she had been summoned to accompany Amelie to dinner with Signor Rocceforte. Amelie was here, now, dubiously looking her teacher over.

'Have you not got any cocktail frocks?' Amelie asked her, eyeing the plain navy-blue long-sleeved dress critically.

Jenna shook her head. 'No—and even if I had, I wouldn't dream of wearing one. I'm your teacher, Amelie—an employee—not your father's guest.'

Her eyes went to the little girl, and she tried to keep her expression more neutral than her opinion. It was obvious to Jenna that the child had been treated like a fashion doll by her socialite mother, and tonight Amelie had gone to town. And not in a good way.

Out of her huge designer wardrobe she had chosen a miniature version of an adult cocktail dress, in a vivid fuchsia satin, patterned with gold and black swirls making the initials of the designer—who was

known, even to Jenna, for his gaudy, overblown de-
signs. It was completely unsuitable for a child her
age, but as Amelie twirled happily about Jenna did
not have the heart to say so.

Amelie's father, however, clearly had no such
compunction. As his eyes lit upon his daughter when
they entered the dining room Jenna saw his dark
brows snap together in instant condemnation of her
oversophisticated dress.

'Amelie wanted to wear a party dress to look par-
ticularly nice for you tonight,' she interjected swiftly,
and was relieved that he said nothing, switching his
glance to her instead.

'Unlike yourself, I see, Miss Ayrton,' he replied,
his tone sardonic, his slate-dark eyes flicking over
her modest attire.

She made no answer, for none was required, but
Amelie spoke up instead.

'If I were taller I would lend you one of *my*
frocks!' she said, rising to her defence, and Jenna
was touched by it.

'She may thank the good Lord you are not, then,'
Evandro observed mordantly.

Then, apparently done with the controversial subject, he bade them both to sit down at the table, its
polished mahogany surface now graced with silver
cutlery and crystal glasses.

Despite the formality of the setting in the grandly
appointed dining room, her employer's manner and
appearance were more casual. He'd changed into ele-
gantly cut dark trousers and a grey cashmere sweater.

Even casually dressed, however, he'd lost none of his imposing presence, nor his disturbing ability to draw her eyes to him—which was *irrelevant*, Jenna reminded herself trenchantly.

He reached to put a strong, square-palmed hand around the bottle of wine that was breathing in a silver holder.

'Do you drink wine, Miss Ayrton, or is that against your principles when in the company of your students?' he enquired, with a lift of one dark brow. There seemed to be a quizzical, almost challenging note to his voice, and a mordant glint in his dark eyes.

'If you have no objection, then nor do I,' she returned equably, not rising to his taunt.

He filled a wine glass, passed it to her, then filled a glass with juice for his daughter. Once done, he lifted his own glass, bidding Jenna and Amelie to do likewise.

'*Saluti!*' he announced, then glanced at his daughter. 'That is what we say here in Italy, instead of *Santé*, as they do in France, or *Cheers*, as they do in England. Isn't that right, Miss Ayrton?'

His dark glance came Jenna's way, and she nodded.

'Good,' he pronounced. 'Then drink up!'

He took a draught from his glass, and Jenna took a more modest sip from hers. The wine was rich and heady, and out of nowhere Jenna felt herself relax, realising only as she did so that there had been a tension in her that was a combination of concern for Amelie and—yet again—a sense of self-consciousness about being in the company of her employer.

I can't make him out, with that mix of acerbic wit and good humour, she thought, lowering her wine glass, flicking her eyes towards him as he greeted the arrival of their dinner, served by the two maids. He thanked them, and Jenna suspected that the two young women were as conscious of his brooding, powerful masculinity as she was. As probably all females were.

It was a disquieting thought. She had no business being aware of her employer in any terms other than just that—her employer. Nothing more.

Then a familiar, if bleak, reassurance came to her. It didn't matter a jot what she thought about Evandro Rocceforte—or any other man. Men never really saw her and she was used to that. It was safer that way.

She'd tried, long ago, to be noticed, to be regarded as someone worth noticing, worth paying attention to—and had failed miserably. So it was safer never to try.

Her eyes went to Amelie, the little girl she felt so drawn to. Amelie was glancing at her father, and Jenna could tell she was not entirely at ease. Her father was still such an unknown quantity to her, and it was understandable that she should be uncertain in his company.

I don't want her ever to hunger for her father's attention. To know the hurt of rejection, the kind of loneliness it once condemned me to.

The loneliness she was still condemned to…

She gave herself a mental shake. Self-pity was both objectionable and pointless. She had accepted long ago that she had no appeal to men—and if that made for loneliness, then it was, in its way, protective.

'Buon appetito!'

The deep voice from the head of the table banished her introspective thoughts and she made a start on the beautifully cooked first course—a layered terrine of salmon and seafood bathed in a lobster bisque, garnished with radicchio and rocket, and served with curling melba toast. She glanced towards Amelie, in case the sophisticated dish was more than she could cope with—she had much plainer fare for her meals with Jenna, her teacher. But the little girl seemed undaunted, daintily using the correct fork, neatly demolishing the terrine without question or objection.

'You must bear in mind, Miss Ayrton,' Evandro informed her, as if he'd noticed Jenna's covert observation of his daughter, 'that in Italy—as in France—children are not packed off to bed early, but spend the evenings with their parents, including going out to restaurants.'

'Sometimes Maman let me go out with her and her friends,' Amelie put in. 'I had to wear my best dresses and not chatter, and not make a mess when I ate, or she would get cross with me…'

Her little voice, which had started out brightly, trailed off unhappily, as it so often did when she was recalling her life with her capricious and demanding mother, and Jenna's heart squeezed for her. Automatically she began to say something reassuring, but Evandro was there before her.

'Well, I can see, *mignonne*, that your table manners…' he swapped to Amelie's mother tongue, French, his voice warming approvingly, '…*sont par excellence!*'

Amelie beamed in pleasure at the praise, and Jenna smiled, too, glad for the little girl's sake, and yet feeling a strange pang inside her as well. She could remember no instances of her own father ever praising her for anything at all, however much she'd longed for a kindly word from him.

Knowing such memories were as useless as they were painful, she refocused, becoming aware that the slate-grey gaze from the head of the table was once more directed at her.

'You approve?' he asked pointedly.

'I approve of your approval,' Jenna answered, less pointedly.

If he was asking if she approved of his praising his daughter, in the way he just had, then of course she did. Though why he should seek *her* approval she did not know.

'I shall take that as a singular compliment,' came the reply.

Then he moved the conversation on, speaking to Amelie again, his tone encouraging.

'Miss Jenna tells me you enjoy art, *mignonne*. She showed me some of your pieces this morning.

I would like to see more of them. Will you do a painting for me, hmm?'

Amelie's face lit up, all trace of uncertainty gone. 'Oh, yes! I'll do my favourite kind. Signorina Jenna likes me to paint things like flowers, and things that I imagine, but what I like doing best,' she announced boldly, 'is making fashion pictures. Because fashion is *so* important,' she finished portentously. 'Maman says it's essential to be *toujours à la mode*!'

Jenna saw her employer's face tighten, and poised herself to intervene with a mediatory comment. She did not want Amelie to be slapped down for her remark, or for the child's father to undo the good work he'd done in praising her.

But, despite his tightened expression, she was relieved when all her employer said was, 'Well, in fashion-conscious places like Paris and Milan, yes…'

Jenna could tell he was trying to modulate the tone of his voice so it would have the best effect on Amelie.

'But only when you're grown up. Or at least a teenager,' he finished repressively.

A confused look crossed Amelie's face, as if what he'd said went against everything her mother had taught her. This time, Jenna found herself interjecting. Yes, Amelie had a precociously unhealthy obsession with designer fashion, thanks to her mother's influence, but that could easily be channelled into something far more harmless and far more appropriate for a little girl.

'But what *is* fun at your age,' she said decisively, 'is dressing up! At the school I taught at in London,' she went on, 'every year there was a World Book Day, and all the children dressed up as someone out of a book or story they'd read. Who would you dress up as, Amelie?' she asked, wanting the little girl diverted from the subject of *haute couture*.

'A medieval princess!' she said immediately, not surprising Jenna in the least. 'Like Sleeping Beauty—but after she's woken up!'

'Perfetto!' her father pronounced, and Amelie looked pleased.

Then his dark gaze went to Jenna, and that caustic expression, increasingly familiar to her now, was back on his face as he addressed her, reaching for his wine glass. But there was humour in his expression too. Dark, but definitely there.

'So, tell me, if you will, Miss Ayrton, as the strict teacher that you are, what character would you recommend for me? Should I expect the worst? Or hope for the best?'

There was a decided glint in his eyes that told Jenna this was one of his ironically voiced remarks she was beginning to get the measure of. Calmly she replied, 'Well, I think any ogre would be far too harsh, so perhaps one of the stern kings in a fairy tale, despatching knights in armour on perilous quests?'

He gave a bark of laughter, his mouth twisting. 'And there I was, hoping you might cast me as Prince Charming!'

Jenna frowned slightly as the twist of his mouth increased, becoming almost bitter... She watched as he took yet another drink from his wine glass.

'Perhaps you are,' she heard herself saying quietly, the words seeming to form themselves, 'but in the story you are under a malign spell.'

Something moved in his slate eyes, and the lines around his mouth deepened.

'Cast by an evil enchantress?' he supplied.

Jenna felt in his gaze a weight that was suddenly crushing.

'Can such a spell ever be broken, do you think?' he asked.

'All such spells can be broken,' she answered.

For a moment—nothing more than a moment— her eyes held his. 'But how?' he asked, his voice low, and there was something in it that chilled her, for all this fanciful talk of fairy tales.

Then a new voice spoke up. Amelie's. 'The good fairy always breaks the spell, Papà!'

The dark gaze that had pressed upon her suddenly switched to the little girl, and Jenna felt herself breathe again.

'So, where do I find this good fairy, hmm?' he quizzed, addressing his daughter.

'She floats down in a silver bubble,' Amelie informed him. 'With silver hair and silver wings and a silver wand and a silver dress.'

Jenna saw her charge's face become animated as she described the vision. 'Why don't you paint a picture of her for your *papà*?' she suggested.

'An excellent idea!' Evandro agreed. His voice was jocular once more. 'I shall look forward to seeing it. Now,' he went on, 'if we are all finished with our *primo*, we shall proceed to the *secondo*.'

He pressed a discreet buzzer by his place setting, and within moments the maids had arrived to clear their plates and replace them with lamb fillet in a rich sauce.

Again, Amelie seemed undaunted by the gourmet fare. And also increasingly undaunted, Jenna was glad to observe, by her father's presence. She could see the little girl relaxing, being assiduously drawn out by her father, who was now asking her what she knew of Italy's long history.

Jenna herself said very little, only prompting Amelie from time to time if she sounded unsure, and listening with interest as Evandro elaborated on what his daughter knew, telling tales from history in a calculatedly dramatic fashion to hold Amelie's interest.

The subject lasted through their final course, a delicate pear parfait—which, although delicious, Jenna could see Amelie was struggling to finish.

Her father saw it too. '*Piccolina*, you are falling asleep!' he pronounced. 'Time for your bed!'

Jenna made to rise, but he stayed her.

'No—Loretta or Maria can see to Amelie. I would like adult company with my *formaggio*,' he declared.

When Loretta appeared at his summons, and led a sleepy Amelie away, he bade her goodnight in a gentler voice than Jenna had yet heard him use, speaking in Italian.

'*Dormi bene, piccolina...*' He smiled. 'And dream of silver fairies.'

Then, with Amelie gone, and an extensive cheese platter placed on the table by one of the maids, he turned back to Jenna. For a moment his eyes rested on her, their expression unreadable, and Jenna felt a spurt of awkwardness. It was one thing to dine with her employer in order to keep his daughter company, but to sit here at the table with only him seemed quite different.

His next words made her realise why he'd sent Amelie upstairs with Loretta.

'So,' he said, pushing the cheese board towards her and indicating that she should help herself, 'your judgement, if you please, Miss Ayrton. How have I done so far? Am I anywhere close to meeting your stipulations as regards Amelie?'

Did he actually want to know her thoughts, or was this another of his ironic challenges? It was hard to tell. Hard to know just how to read this darkly enigmatic man, the likes of whom she had never encountered in all her life.

But he was putting her on the spot, and she must answer as required.

'If my opinion holds any validity, Signor Rocceforte, then I would say, very readily, that you are well on the way to building a good relationship with your daughter,' Jenna replied. Her voice warmed.

'I could see Amelie relaxing more and more—especially when you praised her.'

'There is much to praise,' came the reply. Then his expression tightened. 'Except her choice of dress.'

Carefully, Jenna made her selection from the array of *formaggi*, and even more carefully gave her answer.

'I do realise that the majority of Amelie's wardrobe is…unsuitable, but…' she eyed him cautiously '…if fashion is what Amelie's mother was most interested in, then it is only to be expected that her daughter will have sought to gain her mother's favour and approval by copying that interest. It would be unfair to condemn Amelie for—'

'For her mother's sins.'

The voice cutting across hers was harsh, silencing Jenna. She saw him move restlessly in his chair, refilling his wine glass and swirling it moodily. His eyes dropped from Jenna, as if his thoughts were many miles away. Then, abruptly, his gaze lifted to her again, darker than ever.

'My ex-wife's predilection for squandering obscene amounts of money on couture clothes was the least of her sins,' he bit out.

He moved restlessly again, taking another draught from his wine. Jenna got the impression he was exerting a formidable control over himself now, to curb his outburst. Deep emotions were playing beneath that carapace of control. Just how bitter had his divorce been? Jenna found herself wondering.

Then, as if banishing thoughts that brought him displeasure, he said, 'Well, one thing is obvious— a new wardrobe must be purchased for Amelie.' He looked directly at Jenna. 'You must help in the selection—I know nothing about children's clothes.'

'If you wish,' she answered.

'I do wish,' he said imperiously, helping himself to several wedges from the cheese board, and crackers to go with them. A frown creased his brow. 'You were telling me something this afternoon on the terrace,' he said in his abrupt way. 'About the children of divorced parents. Continue, if you please.'

Slowly, she buttered a cracker, not in the least sure that she wanted to do as he bade. But he was clearly waiting for her answer. An answer that might help Amelie if she could make the little girl's father understand it.

Tentatively, she began, feeling her way as she spoke. 'Children can get…lost…in the divide between warring parents. They can become, as I said, invisible. And sometimes…' her voice changed, she could not stop it '…that becomes exactly what the child begins to want '

She broke off, conscious that she had veered into territory she did not want to give voice to. But Evandro, it seemed, was not a man to permit evasion.

'You speak of yourself, I assume?' he said. His gaze narrowed, arrowing down the table at her. 'But why should you want to be invisible?' His expression hardened.

Jenna shook her head. An air of unreality was

swirling about her. Perhaps it was the late hour, or the quietness around them, and the fact that no one else was present. Perhaps that was what made it easier to say what she said now, her voice low, but unflinching.

'When my mother was killed in a car crash I was sent to live with my father and the woman he'd left my mother for. My presence was…not welcomed. Neither by my stepmother and her children—nor by my father.'

His dark, unreadable gaze rested on her. 'How old were you?'

'Younger than Amelie—just six years old.'

She saw his mouth twist.

'I held on, continuing to hope that one day…' she swallowed '…one day my father would…would *see* me. That one day I would stop being invisible to him. But it never happened. And after a while it seemed better to accept that. Safer.'

His dark brows drew together. 'Safer?'

She felt her grip tighten on the cheese knife in her hand. 'Safer not to want what could not be. Safer to stay invisible.'

He nodded, but slowly, his heavy gaze never leaving her. 'And you are still invisible,' he said softly.

She felt it like a blow, which was odd, because she knew very well that she was invisible. Knew she could walk into any room and no one would notice. It was the way she'd come to want it, because it was safer than the alternative. Being condemned for her very existence, as she had when a child.

She sought to clear her head—clear the emotion that had risen up within her at remembering the unhappy childhood she had endured.

As if surfacing from beneath a deep sea, she realised he was speaking again. His voice had changed, become decisive.

'Well, if that is your concern for Amelie, you may set your anxiety at rest. Amelie is very, very visible to me, I assure you. And I will be doing all in my power, as you admonished me to do this morning, to make her feel wanted and valued. Because, Miss Ayrton, I promise you that nothing will take her from me. *Nothing.*'

There was a vehemence in his voice and a grim determination in his face that made her look at him, setting aside her own troubling recollections.

His avowal should surely be welcome to her, dissipating her fears for Amelie, the little girl uprooted to a new home, a new parent. Yet for a moment, nothing more than a moment, his vehemence and determination seemed to chill her.

Then, in the abrupt fashion she was beginning to get used to, his mood changed.

'But enough of grim topics,' he said. 'Tell me, if you please—for you doubtless know better than I—does Amelie like swimming? The weather is getting warm enough to start enjoying the pool. And what else have you discovered that she enjoys—or does not?'

Grateful for the return to easier topics, Jenna provided what answers she could to his questions, continuing until the maid returned, saying Amelie was tucked up in bed, and asking for the *signorina* to come and say goodnight to her.

Jenna took it as an excuse to withdraw. And as she bade her employer goodnight she saw his dark gaze flicker over her as he nodded his reply, as enigmatic as it was brief.

Only later, back in her sitting room after Amelie was asleep, did she find herself wondering how on earth she had come to say what she had to him about her childhood, about what ran so very deep within her. Things she had never spoken about before—let alone to a man like him.

A man whose softly spoken words echoed anew in her head…

Still invisible.

She gave a dismissive shake of her head—as dismissive as his words—and reminded herself of the home truths she should not forget.

Of course she was invisible to him. A man not only of wealth and power, but of formidable dark good looks, who surely would expect—and receive—the eager attentions of the most beautiful and beguiling of women. Women to whom she was the very antithesis.

To such a man as that, what else could she be but invisible?

What else could she want to be…?

Memory rose in her head of how she'd lain in that sensuous, too-relaxing bath last night, entertaining fantasies she'd had no business entertaining. Fantasies of slate-dark eyes resting on her...

She pushed the memory forcibly from her head. It was as inappropriate as it was pointless to think like that about a man who was like none she had ever encountered before.

In the elegant dining room, Evandro sat back in his chair, poured himself a cognac and, his eyelids half closed, rested his gaze on the foot of the table, where Miss Ayrton had been sitting.

Invisible, she'd called herself.

He pondered the word. It was the very opposite of what Berenice was. She was no more capable of being invisible than a peacock. But then, of course, a preening peacock was exactly what she was. A self-obsessed narcissist who required everyone to indulge her, to desire her, to fall under her malign spell.

A malevolent enchantress, indeed. She had destroyed whatever he'd been of a youthful Prince Charming.

He reached for his glass, strctching out his long legs and recalling that exchange over dinner about fairy-tale characters, hearing his own voice asking how evil spells could be broken.

Amelie's piping voice played in his head. *'The good fairy always breaks the spell, Papà.'*

His expression changed. Did such a being exist?

More memories flickered in the tawny cognac, fuelling his senses, playing out myths and legends, fairy tales and folklore. Then into his head came the throwaway remark he'd made to the woman who had appeared out of nowhere in front of his speeding car.

'You look more like some kind of woodland sprite...'

He frowned. She had been foolhardy indeed to risk her life like that—but she seemed to have thought nothing of it.

Just as she thought nothing of standing up to me and telling me my responsibilities to Amelie—not with bombast or vehemence, but with quietly spoken, intent determination that I should hear what she was telling me.

And now he knew why. He could understand now, after the sorry tale of her own childhood, why she felt so strongly about what she had urged him to do.

His meandering thoughts came full circle.

Invisible—is that what she is?

It was hard not to concur. There was nothing about her to draw his eye, his interest. He ran a catalogue of items through his head, recalling her nondescript appearance.

Mid-brown hair, drawn back into a plait, no make-up to enhance her face, and nor did that plain dress and those low-heeled shoes enhance her figure.

She purposely did nothing to draw any attention to herself. Wanting, indeed, to be invisible.

As he took a slow mouthful of the rich cognac he thought again that there was something about her—not just the self-effacing way she looked, but something in the way she spoke to him, answered him, and looked at him with those clear hazel eyes of hers. Something that—

That what?

The question hung in the air, unanswered.

CHAPTER FIVE

JUST AS HE had told Jenna he would, Evandro took time every day to be with Amelie.

He did so unapologetically, interrupting lessons to whisk Amelie off with him—sometimes down to the pool for swimming, sometimes off in his monster of a car to see the latest children's movie in the nearby town, or to go sightseeing, or to a store to add to the growing toy collection in the little girl's playroom. One expedition had seen them return with a pink bicycle, upon which Amelie had proceeded to hurtle along the terrace and the garden paths, much to her delight.

Jenna could only be glad for her, however disrupted her lessons were. Before her eyes she could see Amelie gaining in confidence with her father—and he with her. It warmed her to see it, and to see the efforts he was making to build a loving relationship with his daughter.

A little catch formed in her throat. She must not be envious of Amelie... And yet when she watched the little girl run happily to her father and be caught up by him in a hug, then set off with him for another outing, she was aware that envy was, indeed, what she was feeling.

And something else too. Something she had not expected. Could not explain. Had never felt the force of before.

All her life she had made herself content with her own company—yet now, as she waved Amelie off on another excursion with her father, she could feel the pluck of loneliness inside her.

She should not be feeling it, she knew—had no business to feel this way. Amelie was her pupil and Evandro was her employer. This beautiful *palazzo* was only her temporary place of work. And yet for all her reminders of how she was only passing through, she was aware that, however occupied she kept herself—swimming lengths in the pool when Amelie and Evandro were away, going for walks in the woods and planning her pupil's next set of lessons—her customary solitude was not welcome any more.

It was a strange, unsettling feeling to be unsatisfied with her own company. To wonder what Amelie and her father were doing together. To miss the little girl's constant company. To realise—and this was most unsettling of all—that the highlight of her day was coming to be the brief exchanges she had with Evandro on the evenings when she accompanied her pupil to dine with him.

She found herself looking forward to those times. Looking forward to that mix of outspoken directness and sometimes caustic, sometimes straight-faced humour that he could bring to any exchange. Found that as the days passed she was becoming more and more at ease in his company.

She wondered at it, trying to find an explanation. After all, a man like Evandro Rocceforte was utterly removed from her own world—wealthy, cosmopolitan, a man of high corporate affairs. A man who surely could find little to interest him in a woman like herself.

And yet after they had dined, and Amelie had been despatched upstairs to be put to bed, Evandro would lean back in his chair, extend his long legs under the dining table, refill their glasses and start a conversation with Jenna that had nothing to do with his daughter. It might be about current affairs, or Italian art, or works of literature—or any other topic of his choosing.

'Speak plainly, if you please, Miss Ayrton,' he would say, reaching for his wine glass and levelling his mordant gaze at her. 'I would have your honest opinion. Come, I know that you have one—and very likely a trenchant one at that. However quietly you speak, you will skewer the subject. I have come to expect nothing less.'

It was curious, Jenna thought. As perpetually aware as she was of the formidable presence of Evandro, when it came to conversing with him she was finding it a heady experience. One she was not used to at all.

Evandro, when his unnerving slate-dark gaze settled on her and his deep-timbred voice addressed her, required her to respond to him. He would not let her be reticent, and she—and this was the most unsettling thing of all—was becoming increasingly and disquietingly aware that perhaps she did not wish to be reticent. She found it mentally stimulating—invigorating, even—to have her opinions sought and listened to.

The days passed, and although Jenna was no longer needed to act as any kind of bridge between Amelie and her father, Evandro repeatedly invited her to join them for lunch, as well as dinner, or on another nature walk, or a ramble through the woods, or—much to Amelie's excitement—to help when he set the ornamental fountain working.

Another realisation slowly built up in her—a realisation that changed all her boundaries, all her expectations, and created, in their place, a hunger to behave differently from the way she had always lived her life. To reject all that she was familiar with, comfortable with, safe with.

She was wishing, for the first time in her life, something she had never wished before.

I don't want to be invisible any more.

Not to Evandro Rocceforte.

'*Piccola*, Signora Farrafacci says she is going to teach you to make cookies this afternoon,' Evandro announced at lunchtime. He turned to Miss Ayrton. 'So you and I,' he said, 'shall go for an energetic walk through the woods. You dawdle, *mignonne*,' he threw at Amelie with a smile. 'Enjoy your cookie-making instead.'

Jenna started to make some protest about the proposed walk, but he overrode her.

'No—no retreating to your sitting room, if you please. I require both exercise and good conversation, and only you will do for both.'

Just why only she would do he was not prepared, at this juncture, to waste time examining. Jenna Ayrton might be badly dressed, determined to downplay her appearance, and altogether devoid of any obvious sex appeal, but that had nothing to do with why he wanted to spend time with her. However much he was prioritising time with Amelie, he was also deriving a surprising degree of enjoyment from the company of her teacher—company he was increasingly seeking.

He found he was looking forward to such times— to conversing with a woman the likes of whom he had never encountered before. A woman who, self-effacing as her nature was, he could see was becoming more easy in his company day by day. And he was glad to see it—glad to see her reticence ebbing away under his refusal to let her retreat behind it, glad to see her manner relaxing more and more when she was with him, glad that her smile was readier.

Not everyone found him easy company. His years with Berenice had scarred him, he knew, with a stab of bitterness. Prince Charming had been lost long ago. Now he knew he could be brusque and impatient, peremptory and cynical. But somehow—and he did not really know why, only that it was so—with Jenna Ayrton he seemed to be lifted and lightened.

Perhaps it was because she'd shown she was unfazed by it—perfectly prepared to stand up to him for what she thought was right when it came to Amelie, wanting to guard her against the misery she'd endured in her own sad childhood. Perhaps, too, it was because she seemed to instinctively understand his sardonic sense of humour, responding to it with limpid ripostes of her own that always drew a satisfied smile of acknowledgement from him.

And perhaps most of all, he was coming to realise with a growing awareness, it was because she never answered him without honesty, sincerity or candour. He knew he could trust that what she said, she meant. She never trimmed her answers to fit his views, nor sought to alter his, just accepted the differences between them with untroubled tranquillity.

She holds her own—stands her ground. She answers me rationally, yet with a quiet conviction that can silence me. Just as she silenced me that first morning with her impassioned plea for Amelie. She says what she feels, what to her is right. She puts nothing on—there isn't a shred of artifice about her. With her, what I see is what she is.

His expression darkened, his mouth tightening.

The very opposite of the woman I married...

His eyes shadowed. Was that the reason for Jenna Ayrton's appeal to him? And if it was, then—

For a moment...just a moment...he felt unease furrow his brow—then discarded it. Why recall his lawyer's warnings? How could they possibly apply? Jenna Ayrton was Amelie's teacher, here for the summer only, and if he found enjoyment in her company it was for the sake of her conversation, because of her natural interest in the little girl she was here to teach—the child who was now safe from the malign machinations of her mother. To give the slightest heed to his lawyer's warning would be absurd.

Now, as he set a vigorous pace through the steep wooded hillside, he glanced back at the woman who was so unlike his toxic ex-wife—unlike, come to that, any of the woman he'd celebrated his freedom from Berenice with. She was a good few steps behind him, but not lagging.

'When I was younger,' he remarked, 'I used to run through the trails here, and as a boy I had a treehouse, where I would hide out. I might get it rebuilt for Amelie. Would she like that, do you think?'

'I'm sure she'd love it,' Jenna replied. 'Any child would.'

'And you? Would you have loved a treehouse?' he enquired, throwing another glance at her.

'Oh, yes,' was her answer.

It did not satisfy him. He paused in his stride, letting her catch up. 'Is that all? You know I am not content with monosyllables.'

She looked away, through the cathedral of trees. 'It would have been a good place to hide,' she said. 'My step-siblings resented my presence in their home, so I learnt to keep out of their way. A treehouse would have been ideal for that. As it was, I had to make do with cowering behind the garden shed, where it was full of brambles and nettles, hiding there for hours sometimes, frightened they would find me and delight in taunting and tormenting me.'

There was a bleakness in her face as she looked back into her miserable childhood—the kind of childhood she had feared Amelie might be similarly doomed to had he himself turned out to be cut from the same cloth her callous father obviously had been.

His mouth set. Well, Amelie's childhood was safe now. There was no question—*none*—of anything else. But as for her teacher…

He had probed into her wretched childhood, confronted the misery she'd endured—the misery that had reaffirmed for him how absolutely essential it had been for him not to condemn Amelie to the custody of an unloving parent. But the misery still cast a pall over her. Haunting her. Blighting her.

Evandro rapidly marshalled the thoughts in his head, rearranging them in a way he had not seen, had not expected, shaping them into a new, fast-strengthening resolve.

His eyes went to her. The dappled sunlight played on her light brown hair, loosened from its plait by the hard-paced walking and forming tendrils that softened her features. Her cheeks had become flushed by exertion, her hazel eyes were made green by the canopy of leaves overhead, and her slight breasts were lifted by her faster breathing after their hike. Into his head came, once again, the description he'd given her during that first dramatic encounter by the deadly rockfall.

A woodland sprite... A sylph of the forest...who might vanish away into the forest's depths, unseen.

Invisible.

As invisible as her callous father had made her feel.

As invisible as she still thought herself.

Evandro's eyes flashed with sudden intensity. Sudden decision.

I don't want her to be invisible. Not any longer. Not to herself.

Nor to me.

The added thought came into his head unbidden, but he quickly banished it.

CHAPTER SIX

EVANDRO RESTED HIS elbow in relaxed fashion on the rim of the open driver's window of the sleek, silver-grey saloon car which carried the three of them far more comfortably than the low-slung supercar he'd arrived in. He was waiting for his passengers to emerge from the *palazzo* and he was looking forward to the day ahead.

Ostensibly the outing was to buy new, far more suitable clothes for Amelie, but there was something else he had every intention of achieving today.

His eyes glinted, satisfaction filling him.

His glance went to the front door, and he was rewarded by its opening and two figures coming out. Amelie—wearing a sequinned pink top and a yellow puffball skirt, thereby demonstrating to him the absolute necessity of a new wardrobe—ran forward as he got out to open the rear passenger door for her with a deliberate flourish, restricting his comments on her dire appearance to say only that she looked so dazzling he would need sunglasses.

She clambered in, settling herself on the booster

seat, and he checked her safety belt was secure before turning back to Jenna.

She was looking, he noticed immediately, somehow less plain this morning. Perhaps because they were going out for the day.

The light blue shirt dress she was wearing looked surprisingly neat on her, with its narrow belt emphasising her small waist and its lapels—whether she was aware of it or not, and he suspected she was not—drawing attention to the discreet swell of her breasts beneath the prosaic cotton of her bodice.

And although, as usual, she had not a scrap of make-up on, there was a glow in her eyes, and in her complexion, that was also perhaps due to the prospect of the day out ahead.

Whatever the cause, he welcomed it.

Firmly, he closed the rear passenger door of the car. He had no intention of letting her sit beside Amelie in the back.

'I want you here, beside me,' he declared, gesturing to the front passenger seat, 'so that I may point out the sights. You've been cooped up far too long, so we shall be combining shopping with sightseeing.' He threw a glance at her as she complied with his wishes and settled herself in the front. 'It's time you saw something of the region.'

'There really is no necessity to take me sightseeing—' Jenna began, making a predictable objection to his plans, but he overrode it briskly.

'We'll also be including a visit to a nearby Roman villa—a notable archaeological site, which I'm sure will be sufficiently educational for Amelie, in case you have any reservations about her taking a day off.' He gunned the engine. 'And now...*avanti*!'

He swept off in a spray of gravel towards the narrow drive that dropped steeply down to the highway below. The memory of Jenna running into the path of his car to stop him hitting the rockfall sprang vivid in his head and he turned towards her.

His tone as he spoke was different from his earlier light-hearted pronouncement. Serious now...sombre. 'I never thanked you for what you did back then—only yelled at you. You most likely saved my life.'

A sudden cold filled him.

If I'd died then—smashed myself to pieces—Amelie would have been returned to Berenice, doomed to grow up twisted and distorted like her mother, either to become as selfish and as narcissistic as she is, or else hurt and damaged beyond measure, forever craving a love the woman is incapable of.

It was a thought beyond bearing.

'So, belatedly, I thank you now,' he said.

Jenna's eyes met his, and in that moment there was a sudden intensity, even if it lasted only a fraction of a second.

And as he pulled his focus back to the narrow road, the moment reverberated in his head.

'Pasta for *pranzo*!' Evandro declared as they settled themselves down at one of the outside tables of a trattoria in the *piazza* of the ancient medieval hill-top town where they'd stopped to eat lunch.

The day so far had been wonderful—Jenna had enjoyed it all. First, they'd gone to see the excavated Roman villa, where Amelie had admired the mosaics and her father had explained the hypocaust heating system to them both, and then they'd driven on through the rolling countryside, past cornfields and vineyards, and stately cedars marching along the roads, with Evandro pointing out sights of historic and geographical interest, telling them about wine production and how people had lived in the past, and tales of famous and heroic figures.

Whether or not Amelie had taken it all in, Jenna wasn't sure, but it was all part of her learning curve, and it brought to vivid life the lessons she'd had in the schoolroom.

As for herself, she couldn't deny how enjoyable it was to see the wider countryside of this part of Italy—which she had never previously visited—and nor could she deny how enjoyable it was be included. Or how enjoyable it was to feel so comfortable as she did now with Evandro.

She replayed in her head the way he'd thanked her for stopping his car from crashing into the rockfall, his voice so sombre. The way he'd looked at her as he'd spoken had had something about it that had stilled her with its intensity. But then it had gone, and his attention had been on his driving again.

Her eyes went to him now, as he discussed the pasta options with Amelie, their heads bent together over a menu, one so dark and one so fair. A memory plucked at her of how she'd wondered from which side of her parentage Amelie had got her blond hair and fair colouring. But what did it matter? Her expression softened as she watched the two of them, so natural together now, so completely at ease with each other.

Her fears for Amelie had been completely eliminated.

She will never be the lonely outcast with no place to belong that I was.

She felt her throat tighten. Was that not still true for her? However lovely it was to be taken out like this, to be on such easy terms with the man who employed her, to be so fond of the little girl who was her pupil, to be so glad that the child and the father were building a close, mutually affectionate relationship, she herself was only an outsider—an observer.

I'll be gone by the autumn and I'll likely never see them again.

The thought was like a needle, piercing her, and the sharpness of it shocked her.

She seized a menu, making herself focus on the contents. Yes, her time in Italy would end—her time with Amelie at the beautiful *palazzo* and her time with Evandro.

But till then... Till then she would enjoy all that she had here.

'Are we going shopping now?'

Amelie's hopeful voice piped up as they got back

into the car. After a leisurely lunch, they'd gone to look inside the church in the *piazza*—famed locally, Evandro had informed Jenna, for its *quattrocento* murals. Though Amelie had enjoyed lighting a candle to the Madonna and the Infant Jesus, she was keener on heading off to the shops for the promised shopping expedition.

'Yes, you little magpie, we are!' her father confirmed, and they set off, leaving the picturesque hilltop town and heading towards the largest town of the region, which had a sizeable shopping district, including a department store, where they parked.

Once in the children's clothes section, Amelie ran gleefully forward.

'And now,' Evandro informed Jenna ruthlessly, 'I shall leave you to it. Get her everything she needs. And make sure you include a couple of dressier pieces that are preferable alternatives to her current appalling collection,' he finished grimly. 'I'll be back in an hour to pay.'

Then he was gone.

The hour, naturally enough, flashed by, and by dint of steering Amelie's pleasurable indecision with her gently firm guidance, Jenna helped her select a sufficient number of suitable garments.

On the dot, her father reappeared.

'Much better,' he said approvingly of Amelie's simple gingham sundress, promptly paying for it and all the other purchases with the flick of a very exclusive-looking credit card.

Then he hunkered down beside Amelie and spoke

to her in a low, conspiratorial tone. Amelie's eyes lit up, and she nodded vigorously.

Evandro straightened, hefting up the plentiful carrier bags. 'Now it's your turn,' he said to Jenna.

She stared. 'I don't understand.'

'Amelie wants you to have a new dress,' he informed her, his voice as smooth as butter. 'To say thank you for all the maths lessons.'

Amelie tugged at Jenna's hand. 'It isn't really for the maths lessons,' she told her. 'Because I don't like maths and I would rather not have maths lessons, so Papà is only teasing. But it *is* to say thank you.' She was gazing up at Jenna. 'It's a present from me,' she said. Uncertainty hovered in her face suddenly. 'If…if you *want* a present from me…' Her little voice trailed off, her eyes anxious.

It was impossible to refuse—unthinkable.

Jenna caught Amelie's other hand and squeezed both tightly. 'I'd *adore* a present from you,' she said warmly. 'And a new dress would be absolutely *lovely*.'

How could she possibly reject the little girl? Even though she'd been ruthlessly—shamelessly— manoeuvred into this by Evandro, for whatever amusement that it might afford him. Though for the life of her she could not imagine why, unless it was an act of casual lordly benevolence… Or maybe— and more likely, she thought with her customary painful honesty—it was masculine revulsion at being seen out with a female who was so utterly unlike any kind of female he'd have chosen for companionship.

Amelie's face had lit up at her fulsome reply and, consigning herself to her fate, Jenna let herself be led towards the womenswear department.

She'd fully expected her employer to disappear again, but he deposited himself in one of the large leather armchairs positioned for the convenience of those males haplessly corralled into clothes shopping, and availed himself of the several sporting magazines provided to lessen the grim ordeal.

Amelie, happily in her element again, marched Jenna up and down the racks of clothing until she found one that displayed what she was after.

'These are like my dresses, but in your size,' she told Jenna, starting to rifle through the display.

A shop assistant glided up and joined in enthusiastically.

Jenna gave in, defeated.

Evandro logged off his computer, all the work he'd intended to do today satisfactorily completed. His senior executive team was happy, his shareholders were happy, his clients were happy, his project managers were happy—and he was happy.

He sat for a moment, wondering at that. Wondering that he should be happy at all. It wasn't an emotion he was used to. Not for years. Then, getting to his feet, he stopped wondering, and simply enjoyed the sensation.

He glanced at his watch—four o'clock. Time for afternoon tea. A very special afternoon tea—a tea *party*, in fact. With everyone looking the part.

Including Jenna Ayrton, who would be wearing the new dress he'd shamelessly manoeuvred her into accepting.

He'd done so quite deliberately.

As they'd walked through the woods that day he'd resolved not to let her be invisible any more. Not to let her be haunted by her miserable childhood. He didn't want her endlessly hiding from the world, tucking herself away, out of sight, thinking so harshly of herself...

And now he would see what his scheming had achieved. He'd given Amelie strict instructions that morning—instructions that had made her eyes light up gleefully and enthusiastically—and now, as he strolled out of the library, his eyes went to the wide marble stairway descending into the hall.

And there they were. Amelie and Jenna. Coming down the stairs.

Amelie looked as pretty as a picture in one of the new dresses purchased the previous day, with her long golden hair held back by a floral Alice band that had a bow on it to match the yellow sash of her full-skirted dress with its delicate pattern of little yellow roses. She was beaming widely, sedately holding Jenna's hand, and Evandro felt something clutch at him to see her smiling so trustingly at him, filling him with an emotion that gripped him with an intensity he had never felt so fiercely.

She was safe here, with him to look after her as best he could. And he would keep her safe—for her sake and for his own. The child who had been deliberately kept from him, deliberately used as a weapon against him, was a stranger no longer.

He felt his heart clench with protectiveness... with love.

I may have no qualifications to be a father, and I may have had to feel my way, day by day, to win her confidence, her trust, but now...

In his head he heard the words that Jenna had spoken to him.

Every child should be valued, wanted...loved.

Emotion welled in him as Amelie, letting go of her teacher's hand, ran up to him.

And she is all of those—all of them. Valued, wanted...and loved.

He stooped to hug her, feeling her little arms wind about his neck, feeling again that welling of emotion inside him. Then he stood up, his eyes going to Jenna.

Por Dio!

She was not invisible at all.

Like a woodland sprite...

The words popped into his head of their own accord as his gaze rested on her, unable to tear itself away. Her slender figure was as graceful as a dryad's in the soft green of her ballerina-length, fifties-style dress, with its gathered skirt and the sweetheart neckline that ruched over her shoulders, left her arms bare, emphasised her tiny waist.

For the first time she was wearing her hair loose, in the same style as Amelie, held back softly from her face with a green velvet ribbon. As for her face...

His eyes glinted. She was wearing make-up. Not much—a little mascara, some smoky eyeshadow to deepen her eyes, turned now to a forest-green like her dress, and a touch of lip gloss to bring a sheen to her curving mouth—but it was enough for him to see that her delicate features would draw the male eye as they had never drawn it before...making it want only to appreciate...to linger...

Then Amelie was speaking to him, her voice eager. 'Do we look nice, Papà, Miss Jenna and me?'

'You look enchanting!' he said promptly. 'Both of you!'

He worked his eyes over Jenna once more, knowing it made her colour heighten, and glad of it.

'At last,' he said softly, stepping forward. 'You have come out of hiding. Made yourself visible.' He took her hand, which seemed to quiver in his, and raised it to his lips in a formal, stately fashion. 'Never hide again,' he said quietly, for her alone.

For a moment he held her gaze, and something— he did not know what—seemed to change in the world around him. Inside him. Something that he had not known could change...

In his head, like a poisoned dart shot at him from far away, he heard his lawyer's words of foreboding. He shook them out, refusing to acknowledge them or let them penetrate the strange emotion filling him now, which seemed to permeate him with a warming glow.

Jenna's slender hand was still in his, cool beneath his fingers. He tucked it into his arm, did the same with Amelie's hand, and led them both forward with a smile.

'And now that I have a *bella donna* on either arm—what a lucky dog I am—it is time,' he announced, with satisfaction and triumph in his voice, 'for our tea party.'

'Party' was certainly the word for it, Jenna conceded. Just as she'd had to concede there had been no way out of Amelie's excited, gleeful insistence that she must wear her lovely new dress today and put on make-up for the occasion.

Just as she had in the department store, Jenna had given in. She had not been able to disappoint Amelie, who had been visibly thrilled to be dressing up, and thrilled at the thought of her teacher dressing up too. So she'd left her hair loose, borrowed a ribbon from Amelie's vast collection, and then, with trepidation and Amelie's enthusiastic guidance, made up her face. Not too much, but just enough.

Enough to make my eyes look larger, smokier, my lashes longer, and to give a soft sheen to my lips.

And somehow, though she didn't really understand how, wearing her hair loose seemed to set off her cheekbones and reveal the delicate contours of her jaw that she'd never noticed. The beautifully cut fifties-style dress also seemed to enhance her slight figure, giving her a shapeliness she had not thought she possessed.

She'd stared at her reflection wonderingly. The experience was very different from her feelings when she had examined her unexciting workaday appearance that first night she had been summoned to dine with Amelie and her father.

How different she looked now!

She gazed, trying to take it all in. Trying to remember when she'd last worn make-up, last made any attempt to style her hair attractively, last worn something that might pass for fashionable. At uni, probably, some freshers' bash. Useless, though, because no one took notice of quiet, dull females whom even their own fathers had no interest in, and who were focused only on their studies, not on their social lives. And, as a teacher, all that was needed was for her to look neat and sensible, capable of keeping order in an overcrowded class with more than its fair share of children from disturbed backgrounds and impoverished families.

It was a life a world away from this beautiful, elegant Italian *palazzo*—a world away from the likes of Evandro Rocceforte.

She gave a little tremble now, as she felt her hand hooked around his strong forearm and walked into the rose garden with him and Amelie, where a pretty ironwork table had been set out under a shady parasol.

Had Evandro really swept his slate-dark eyes over her, taken her hand and kissed it as if he were Prince Charming himself?

And I Cinderella...

A Cinderella who had buried herself in her work. Hidden. Invisible.

'Never hide again.'

She heard his voice, low-pitched, intense, and a sense of wonder filled her at how she had found herself wishing, for the first time in her life, for something she had never wished before.

Not to be invisible any longer.

Not to Evandro Rocceforte.

CHAPTER SEVEN

'WELL,' ANNOUNCED EVANDRO'S housekeeper, 'this is a treat!'

Evandro gallantly ushered her to her seat as she sailed into the rose garden, resplendent in a sky-blue skirt and jacket with a jabot blouse, her hair freshly styled.

'Signora Farrafacci has created our repast...' Evandro smiled at Jenna '...so I think it only fair that she should enjoy it with us.'

'Well, I'm a dab hand at a Victoria sponge, if I say so myself,' his housekeeper agreed comfortably.

She beckoned Loretta and Maria forward, each carrying laden trays, which they deposited on the table, adding to what had already been set out.

It was a full English afternoon tea, with gold-rimmed porcelain plates bearing wafer-thin finger sandwiches—Jenna spotted egg, smoked salmon and cucumber—and a display of cakes that made her dizzy with indecision. The icing-sugar-dusted Victoria sponge, oozing raspberry jam from between the layers, looked as resplendent as its creator, and was

flanked by rainbow-hued fairy cakes thick with colourful buttercream icing, and there was a far more
sophisticated gateau St Honoré, made of choux pas-
try and golden spun sugar.

And as for what to wash it all down with—tea
itself was the very least of it...

'What tea party would be complete without champagne, hmm?' quizzed Evandro, lifting the bottle
nestling in its ice bucket by the table and opening it
with a practised easing of the cork.

Champagne was ideal for the occasion. An occasion he'd created and orchestrated to perfection. His
mood was excellent—beyond excellent. Everything
had worked out just as he'd planned.

His eyes went to Jenna, revelling again in the
transformation he had wrought in her. Goodbye,
sad, haunted ghost of her miserable childhood, and
welcome—oh, very, *very* much welcome—to the
woman he had made reveal herself.

His gaze softened again in satisfaction and a wry,
appreciative bemusement. Who would have thought
a dress would make such a difference? A hairstyle?
A touch of make-up? But there was more to it than
that, he knew. It was a new glow that was about her,
a light in her eyes, a smile on her lips that came
from within.

*She knows she is no longer invisible. It is that
that makes the difference. That which draws my eye
to her—*

He cut off his wandering thoughts. The transformation he had wrought in Jenna was for herself, not for him. It was essential to remember that.

Swiftly, he reached for the champagne flutes, filling three of them to the brim and handing one each to Signora Farrafacci and to Jenna, keeping one for himself. Then he reached for another flute and poured in a quarter of a glass, topping it up generously with fresh orange juice and bestowing it upon Amelie.

'This, *mignonne*,' he informed her solemnly, 'is the only fizzy drink it is civilised to consume!' He glanced at Jenna. 'Do not be alarmed—as I said to you earlier, here in Italy, as in France, as well as becoming accustomed to dining out, children are exposed to wine from an early age, but in very small quantities.' He looked back at Amelie. 'Well, what do you think of it?'

The little girl took a cautious sip and wrinkled her nose. 'It tickles!' she said. 'But it's lovely and orangey.'

'It's called a Buck's Fizz,' Signora Farrafacci informed her. 'But I prefer mine straight, thank you very much,' she said, raising her glass to her employer.

He watched as Jenna hastily did likewise.

'*Saluti!*' he exclaimed, and clinked his glass against theirs and Amelie's. 'And now,' he pronounced, entirely and completely satisfied with what he had achieved, 'the feast may begin!'

His gaze washed one more time over the woman he had released from invisibility, who could now finally, belatedly, take her due place in the world, no longer barring herself from what she was entitled.

Signora Farrafacci did the honours, pouring cups of tea for everyone, though Amelie stuck with her Buck's Fizz.

Evandro sat back, a smile on his face. 'How exceptionally pleasant this is,' he announced expansively. 'We should do this more often—all through the summer, even. And we shall all—what is that strange expression?—wear our best bib and tucker when we do so.' He frowned. 'What in heaven is a tucker?'

'I've no idea,' Jenna confessed with a laugh. 'I shall look it up!'

'Well, all I know,' quipped Signora Farrafacci, 'is that I can't wait to *tuck* in!' Which brought a giggle from Amelie.

So they did, and as Jenna sipped at her champagne it was as if the bubbles were seeping into her bloodstream, lifting her into a state of light-heartedness and enjoyment that brought a constant smile to her face.

The convivial atmosphere was led by Evandro, reinforced by Signora Farrafacci's good-hearted joviality, and most of all buoyed by Amelie's stream of giggles and beaming smiles.

Moved, Jenna swept her eyes over the scene, wonderingly.

This is the very definition of happiness.

Her eyes went to the man sitting opposite her, genially teasing his daughter and praising his housekeeper for the excellence of her magnificent Victoria sponge. She could not stop them and had no wish to, she realised, and the welling of happiness within her became radiant.

She could not take her eyes from him. His strong, powerful body relaxed back in the ironwork chair, and the open neck of his pristine white shirt and the turned-back cuffs acknowledged the warmth of the afternoon, all emphasising the masculine strength of his body.

This was the man who had wrought this transformation in her, brought her out of her lifelong hiding from the world—from men. The one man in all the world to whom she was no longer invisible.

Rich, warm, wonderful happiness filled her to the brim—like the sparkling, effervescent champagne in her glass.

'Well, I've eaten my fill and no mistake!' Signora Farrafacci announced. She got to her feet. 'And now I must be off—I'm visiting my son tonight.' She nodded at Evandro as he started to stand up as she did. 'No, no, don't get up. Thank you for this first-class tea party. And,' she finished, 'for requesting a cold dinner tonight so I can go out.'

She lifted the remains of her magnificent Victoria sponge, and Evandro encouraged Amelie to take the leftover fairy cakes to the kitchen. Jenna moved to start clearing the table, but Evandro stopped her.

'No, stay awhile. There is still the champagne to finish,' he said lazily. *'Carina,'* he addressed Amelie, 'if you want to play, either choose something that will not risk your new dress or change.'

Amelie nodded, going after Signora Farrafacci and happily helping herself to the icing on one of the remaining fairy cakes as she did so.

Evandro leisurely reached for the champagne bottle and refilled their glasses. 'So...' he looked at Jenna, stretching out his long legs and lounging back in the ironwork chair '...did you enjoy our tea party?'

His quizzical glance got the reaction he'd expected.

'It was a triumph!' Jenna confirmed.

He laughed. 'As is your new dress.' His eyes drifted over her lazily, appreciatively. 'You cannot imagine the difference it makes.'

He saw her lashes drop over her eyes, more forest green than hazel today, reflecting the colour of the dress that was doing so much for her.

'Thank you,' she said, in a low tone.

There was a quiet intensity in her voice that told him the depth of her feelings. Told him what she was thanking him for.

He reached for her hand. Raised it to his mouth, grazed it lightly, then set it back on the table. It seemed to him the right kind of gesture to make. Anything more might—

He pulled his thoughts away. He'd done what he had for Jenna's sake, he reminded himself. *She* was to be the beneficiary—not himself.

He shifted, suddenly restless. 'And I thank you in

return,' he said, his voice half-serious, half-caustic. 'The dress you chose for Amelie, the one that she wore today, is an infinite improvement on what her mother dressed her in.'

A smile lit Jenna's face. 'She looked enchanting—just as you told her,' she said warmly. 'She wants to please you.'

A frown pulled Evandro's brow. 'I don't need her to want to please me.' His voice was harsh suddenly. 'And if that is the impression I am giving her—and you...' he drew a razor-sharp breath '...then my inexperienced attempts at...at fatherhood—' he spoke the word flatly, almost bleakly '—are failing,' he finished tersely.

He saw her expression change—at first to dismay, at his harsh response, and then to its opposite. Warmth and encouragement.

'You are *not* failing!' she exclaimed feelingly. 'You are making a wonderful father. Wonderful!'

Her face worked, and he could see she was searching for words—the right words.

'It is natural for a child to want to please their parents,' she told him, her voice persuasive, 'and if it's mutual, and you want to please her too—as I can see you do, in so many ways when you are together—then it is entirely justified. It is only if it is one-sided that it becomes dangerous. Unhealthy,' she finished, and now it was her voice that sounded bleak.

'And it is unhealthy between adults too,' he bit out. 'Trying to win the love of someone who is incapable of returning it. Falling under their spell.'

'Cast by an evil enchantress...'

The words dropped from Jenna's lips and hung in the space between them. The same words he'd spoken at that first dinner together.

His shadowed eyes rested on her. She was un-readable—and yet all too readable. He did not need to spell out to her just who the evil enchantress in his life had been. She'd had enough malignity in her own life to know the damage that could be done when love of any kind—whether between parent and child or husband and wife—could not be returned because the other person lacked all capability for that most vital of emotions.

'Just so,' he said, and his gaze held hers. Then, abruptly, he reached for his glass, gesturing that she should do the same. 'Come,' he said, lightening his voice determinedly, to banish all shadows and dark-ness, 'let us not waste champagne on morbid memo-ries. My ex-wife is in the past—as is your father. The only power they have over us now is the power we allow them. Nothing more than that.'

He raised his glass, touching it to hers. Knowing that what he had said was a lie for him. Berenice still had the power to poison.

But he would not think of that—not now, not here.

He let his eyes go to Jenna again, still finding her transformation wondrous. There was no danger, surely, in letting his gaze drink her in.

Peaceably, they sipped their champagne, with the heat of the day softening to a gentle warmth. Above them, from the open window of Amelie's playroom, he could faintly hear her talking to her dolls, discussing their fashion choices with them. He gave a resigned half-smile. Perhaps Amelie would end up making a career in fashion.

He said as much to Jenna. She smiled. 'Well, whatever she chooses, it won't require maths, I suspect.'

He laughed. 'What made you study languages?' he asked, curious.

She made a face. 'I had a facility for them, but mostly, I think—with hindsight—I chose them because they opened my horizons to lives other than the one I had.'

'An escape route?' he said, understanding why she'd wanted that.

She nodded. 'Though then I became keen on teaching—and again,' she said with a rueful half-smile, 'that was to encourage children in their abilities as I was never encouraged in mine.' She looked at him, curiosity in her eyes. 'Did you ever have any choice but to take over Rocceforte Industriale?'

'I wanted to,' he replied. 'Perhaps because it's in my blood. But also because—' He stopped for a moment, took a slow mouthful of his champagne. 'Because it pleased my father. Oh, it's not that I sought his love and regard—I had that plentifully. But for the same reason that I—'

He broke off again. The shadow of Berenice was threatening. He set his mouth. Perhaps it would help to say it. After all, if there were anyone he could say it to, it was this woman here, scarred as she was by the cruelty of others.

'For the same reason that I was so glad to marry Berenice. I was all too willing—but it made my father happy too.' He paused again, his mouth twisting. '"The road to hell is paved with good intentions…"'

Restlessly, he drained his champagne, getting to his feet. Damn the woman he'd married so blindly— damn her to the hell she'd put him in!

The hell she still seeks for me.

Determinedly, he shut down his morbid thoughts, refusing to let them spoil this special day.

'Come,' he said, drawing Jenna to her feet. 'If your glass is empty, too, let us take a stroll to work off all these cakes.'

Good mood restored, he led her off.

Leaving Berenice far, far behind. If he could.

Jenna stood out on the terrace. The sun was near to setting, filling the gardens with rich gold light. The tea things had long been cleared away, and they had all spent the last hour or two on the sofa in Amelie's playroom, first watching one of her favourite movies with her, then playing her favourite computer game—both of which had involved medieval princesses, heroic quests and assorted mythical beasts.

It had been fun and relaxed and convivial.

Now Amelie had been handed over to Maria for her bath time, and Evandro had disappeared into the library to check his emails. Loretta had just

brought out an *aperitivo* for them both, after Jenna
had helped her set the table in the dining room and
fetched the cold collation of salads and *antipasti*
that would suffice as dinner after their lavish afternoon tea.

Bidding Loretta goodnight as she went off duty,
Jenna stood gazing out over the vista beyond, feeling still that rich, warm glow of happiness that had
filled her all afternoon.

She turned as she heard Evandro's distinctive step
emerging onto the terrace. Her face lit—she could
not help it.

Was there an answering light in his as he strolled
up to her? In the fading light she could not tell.

He paused by the table and she watched him,
knowing she could not look away. And nor did she
want to, as he casually picked up their cocktails,
then came across to her.

'See what you make of this,' he said genially,
handing her a martini glass. 'It should refresh the
palette after our afternoon champagne.'

She took a cautious sip—it was tart and citrusy—
and, she suspected, more potent than was probably
wise after two glasses of champagne earlier. But
today was a special day and surely, on a day like
this, caution could be set aside. And wisdom too…

'Well?' Evandro enquired with a lift of his brow.

She gave her judgement and he nodded, satisfied.

'We'll toast the setting sun,' he said. His eyes
went to her. 'And more than the setting sun…'

The sunlight was in her eyes and she could not

make out his expression as he spoke—knew only that there was something in his voice that had never been there before. Something that, just as his show of gallantry when he'd kissed her hand as she descended the staircase in her new dress revealing her new self had done, made her tremble slightly.

She turned to watch the sun pool on the horizon and then slip slowly beneath it in a final glory of gold as they sipped their cocktails. Dusk started to gather, and cicadas were giving soft voice in the air all around them. It was a strangely intimate moment.

Thoughts flickered in Jenna's head, then quietened. This was not a time for thinking, or for wondering, least of all for questioning. Only for standing quietly, as the day turned into night. Standing side by side… Evandro and herself…

A sound behind her made her turn. Amelie was at the open French doors of the dining room, wrapped in her dressing gown, her feet in fluffy slippers. Jenna held out her hand to her, smiling, and the little girl ran up, taking it in her warm, small clasp.

Her father smiled down at her. 'We're looking for the first star, *carina*. Can you see it yet?'

Amelie's eyes strained upward, then her little face lit. 'There! There—I see it, Papà! Up there!'

She pointed to where, almost invisible to the naked eye, the first faint star gleamed in a sky that was leaching slowly of its colour.

'So it is!' exclaimed Jenna.

'Clever girl,' said Evandro, taking his daughter's other hand. He caught Jenna's eye and smiled.

A warm smile of companionship and closeness. A smile that seemed to linger…

She felt the glow that had filled her all afternoon well up in her again. Happiness. Just…happiness.

So simple. So precious. So good to feel.

So unknown in her life—till now.

For a moment longer they stood together, watching the star steadily brighten and the sky darken, Amelie between them, holding hands with each of them.

As if we were a family, Jenna thought. *With Amelie my daughter and Evandro my—*

Abruptly, as if Amelie's hand had suddenly become red-hot, she dropped it, stepped away. Appalled at what she'd just thought.

What she'd dared to want…

Softly, Jenna dropped a kiss on the sleeping child's forehead before turning to head back downstairs. The *palazzo* was in silence, its staff all off duty. She slipped noiselessly into the dining room, where Evandro still sat, long legs extended, his empty wine glass in his hand. His expression was shuttered.

He must have sensed her presence because his head turned and he saw her. Did something change in his eyes? She couldn't tell as the light from the wall sconces was so low.

He got to his feet. 'The moon has risen,' he said. 'Come and see.'

Though she was used to his direct manner, there seemed to be a staccato note to his voice now that was different. But then, she thought, frowning slightly, he had been different over dinner as well. As had she, she knew.

The meal had been an informal affair, and although Evandro had been his usual genial self with Amelie, Jenna had felt his glance often flickering towards herself. Was he still taking in how different she looked—how he had wrought such a transformation in her? Making her visible to his eyes. As she had longed to be.

She had been confused, conflicted. Dismayed by what she had allowed herself to think as they'd stood stargazing after sunset. She had found it hard to look at him, to meet his eyes, and yet she'd been burningly aware of his flickering glances. They'd both focused their attention on Amelie, until her reluctant yawns had drawn Jenna to her feet and she'd taken her up to bed.

She followed Evandro out onto the darkened terrace. Her mood was strange, still conflicted. Perhaps she should not have come back downstairs again. Perhaps she should have bidden him goodnight when she'd taken Amelie up to bed. It would have been better…safer…to wait until tomorrow to see him again, when she would be in her workaday clothes, her hair pinned back, her face plain of make-up.

The dangerous thought that had come to her as she had stood hand in hand with Amelie, the child between them—linking them, uniting them—still assailed her. She knew she must not think it. Knew it was only the result of the moment…an after-effect of the day.

A day that had been made for her, created for her, given to her like a wonderful, precious gift—one she would forever be grateful for. A day like no other in her life.

But she must not read into it her own longings. The longings of someone who had never belonged to a warm and loving family—never belonged at all. Someone who had never had anyone to love her—who had had loneliness imposed upon her and who had had to accept it because it was all she had known…all she had expected from life.

But just because she no longer wanted to choose loneliness it did not mean she could have any place here. Or any claim on anyone here.

Not Amelie—*and not Evandro.*

No claim at all—however much her eyes went to him, however burningly aware she was of him as a man with an overpowering physical impact on her that had been there right from the very first moment, that she had never experienced before.

None of that mattered.

I am Amelie's teacher—that is all. And if her father choses to treat me kindly and decently, that does not mean…does not mean…

She felt her throat catch, as if a barb had lodged there suddenly.

That does not mean anything at all.

And yet…

And yet she felt herself longing for it to mean

something. Wishing that it was for *himself* that he had turned her from plain to pretty, from drab to desirable, turned her into the kind of woman who could light up the eyes of a man like Evandro Rocceforte. A man who had given her a gift she had never before received.

She heard again the words he had spoken to her as he had kissed her hand, paid homage to the woman he had revealed.

'Never hide again.'

And she did not want to. Not from him. She wanted him to go on seeing her—now, tonight. Seeing her made lovely by him. *For* him.

I don't want this day to end—not yet.

The longing sang in her head and her eyes went to him—as they always seemed to want to. He had paused on the terrace and was now turning back to her. She felt her throat catch again, but for a different reason now—because her breath seemed to have vanished on the cool night air.

All around them the chorus of the cicadas filled the air, the scent of fragrant flowers perfumed it. He was looking at her, holding out his hand to her. Saying nothing, only waiting for her to accept. She lifted her face, looked up at him. His strong features were shadowed in the night, and she caught the faint scent of his aftershave.

His outstretched hand touched her hair. 'Always wear it long and loose and lovely. It's a crime to hide it with pins.'

There was a smile in his voice as he spoke, but

also something more than a smile. Something that seemed to reach into her, touching her deep within.

With the lightest touch his hand smoothed down the length of her hair. The sensation was so light it was scarcely there, yet it made her tremble. She could not move—not a muscle. Could only stand gazing up at him, eyes wide...so wide...drinking him in...wanting nothing more in all the world but to be here like this. Looking as she did now for him, for this man.

For this man who is like none other in all the world. The man who, alone of all the men in all the world, has the power to make me feel as I feel now.

She tried to remember—hopelessly, uselessly— what she had just told herself. She was his daughter's teacher—only that...

But how could she think that? How could she think that as she stood there, so very close to him, feeling the fall of her hair flowing down her back like a silken river, feeling the soft folds of the skirts of her beautiful dress brushing her bare legs, feeling the night air drift over her shoulders, feeling the smooth material of her bodice shape her rounded breasts?

She felt the silvered moonlight play upon her face, knowing it enhanced the long-lashed smokiness of her eyes and etched the contours of her delicate features, highlighting the softness of her lips as she gazed up at him, eyes wide, filled with all she felt.

Never before had she been so conscious of her body. Never before had she felt she could do as she did now—gaze upon a man whose strong, powerful physique and whose shadowed face were always and for ever imprinted on her consciousness.

In her breast she could feel her heart beating, and the pulse at her throat was alive. She felt her lips parting as if…as if…

'Oh, Jenna…' he breathed, and there was something in his voice that was like a warning.

But was it a warning to her—or to himself?

'Jenna. Don't—'

There was a break in his voice, a sudden starkness in his shadowed face as he seemed to draw back from her. Her eyes distended, filling with dismay at his withdrawal.

She heard her voice, faint and faraway, whispering his name. 'Evandro…'

All her yearning was in the sound of his name—all that she could no longer deny, no longer withhold. From the very first it had been so. And now… Now…

A rasp broke from him, and the flashing of his dark eyes was caught in the silvered moonlight. Something changed in his face… The lines around his mouth lessened, softened…

For one endless moment time stopped and the universe stopped—her heart stopped. He stood immobile, as if riven by the tension that was racking his strong body, keeping it imprisoned. Then, as though breaking free of bonds, he let his long lashes dip over his dark eyes and lowered his mouth to hers.

His kiss was cool and slow.

Her eyelids fluttered shut and she gave herself to him entirely, with all her being, as his mouth moved across hers softly, sensuously. She felt her heart turn over and over...

His hand closed about her waist, drawing her to him, and of their own accord her own hands lifted, pressing against the broad wall of his chest, feeling its muscled strength beneath her fingertips, her palms, delighting in it, glorying in it.

His kiss deepened and instinctively, willingly—oh, so willingly—her mouth opened to his, returning his deepening kiss, feeling the pleasure of his arousing touch lighting a spark within her. His free hand shaped her face, his thumb curving into the tender hollow behind her ear, fingers spearing gently into the fall of her hair as softly and as sensuously as his kiss...and just as wondrously arousing.

She leant into him, felt the hand at her waist splaying broadly, holding her to him as he kissed her, not cool now, but with a building sensuality that made her breathless, helpless... Wanting this... only this...

Nothing else existed in the world—only this moment now, in his arms, his embrace, with his mouth on hers. He was taking her where she had never been—where she longed to go. Where she longed to be always and for ever.

And then, like a sudden blow, he pulled away from her, lifting his hand from her waist, lifting her hands away from him. Stepping back. Moving away.

She reeled, bereft, her eyes flying open, wild and strained. Her heart was beating wildly, hectically.

He towered over her, blocking the moon. 'Go to bed,' he said. His voice was harsh and rough. His expression was closed. 'Go to bed,' he said again. 'This never happened.'

She did not move. Could not. The solid stone of the paved terrace beneath her feet was cold and hard. As cold and hard as his voice. She felt her nails press into the palms of her hands, as if her nails were the tail of a scorpion, stinging her skin, wounding her flesh.

'This never happened—do you understand?'

His voice was a blade now, and something flashed across his face, flaring in his veiled eyes.

'I take full responsibility—it was my doing, not yours, so the blame is mine and the moon's and the stars'. It's the wine I've drunk and anything and everything else you can throw at me. Throw whatever you want—but go.'

She did not cry out or make a noise, nor any sound at all. Only turned and fled. Invisible once again.

CHAPTER EIGHT

EVANDRO PRESSED THE accelerator, urgently wanting
to be back in Turin, at his desk, as fast as the powerful car could take him there. A glance in the rear-
view mirror showed him that his face was grim and
bleak, as if an iron mask were over it.

Dio—how could he have done what he had? Been
so reckless?

Although he had, he acknowledged, courted exactly this kind of danger right from the start.

*But I never thought it was a danger. Never thought
that a woman I didn't look twice at could ever...*

Could ever what? Get under his skin little by little, slowly but surely, day after day?

He'd thought he was safe. But he had come to
want more than their walks and their smiles and
shared laughter. Had come to want her to stop con-
cealing herself behind the protective cloak of invisibility.

*But it wasn't just protecting her—it was protecting
me as well.*

That was the mocking irony of it. He had told

himself he was doing it for *her* sake, not for his—his gift to her, to make her see herself as she could be, not as she thought she must be, blighted by what she had endured as a child.

He had shown her how beautiful she could be—and shown himself in the process.

And that fatal realisation had been his downfall.

I should never have let her come back down after taking Amelie to bed. Never have been insane enough to take her out onto the moonlit terrace—never let her gaze at me with such longing in her eyes...

He had sought to resist—but how could he have found the strength to do so? From the moment she had come down the staircase in that dress, revealed to him as she truly was, no longer hiding from the callous cruelty that had condemned her, he had felt danger pluck at him.

Oh, he had denied it, blanked it out, been a convivial, benevolent host at the tea party—the same relaxed, good-humoured conversationalist he'd come to be in their times together, enjoying her company as he always had. But underneath, a tide had been turning, an awareness had been pulsing, making him want to look at her, take her in, notice every part of how hauntingly lovely she now looked.

A woodland sprite. Lifting her lovely eyes to the stars, to the moon... To me.

And he had kissed her. And been lost.

Lost to all warnings…all danger.

Lost to the danger that he had only truly recognised when she was close, in his arms. The danger that had made him wrest himself from her, set her aside, say such harsh words to her. Send her fleeing.

Leaving him standing there, cursing the moon and the stars and the night, and above all himself.

And cursing the cruel chains Berenice still bound him with...

'Papà has gone!' Amelie's voice was mournful and unhappy, and she was unwilling to settle back into the routine of daily lessons. 'Back to Turin.'

'He has to work, Amelie—he cannot be here all the time,' Jenna answered steadily, though it was an effort to do so.

Misery filled her. And self-recrimination—bitter and galling—at her own folly. Clinging to him when he'd kissed her, kissing him back with such ardency—only for him to push her away from him, reject what had happened.

She had to reject it too. For his sake—and for hers—she had to consign it to nothing more than a tormenting memory and then starve that memory.

But how? Oh, dear God, how? How could she ever forget? Forget being in his arms...forget his kiss? Forget everything that she had felt and longed for? Forget the touch of the man she had fallen in love with—

She froze, horror washing over her. No—no, that could not be. It couldn't!

That was a folly that was unendurable.

FREE BOOKS GIVEAWAY

GET UP TO FOUR FREE BOOKS & TWO FREE GIFTS WORTH OVER $20!

We pay for everything!

YOU pick your books –
WE pay for everything.

You get up to FOUR New Books and
TWO Mystery Gifts...absolutely FREE

Dear Reader,

I am writing to announce the launch of a huge **FREE BOOKS GIVEAWAY**... and to let you know that YOU are entitled to choose up to FOUR fantastic books that WE pay for.

Try **Harlequin® Desire** books featuring the worlds of the American elite with juicy plot twists, delicious sensuality and intriguing scandal.

Try **Harlequin Presents® Larger-Print** books featuring the glamourous lives of royals and billionaires in a world of exotic locations, where passion knows no bounds.

Or TRY BOTH!

In return, we ask just one favor: Would you please participate in our brief Reader Survey? We'd love to hear from you.

This FREE BOOKS GIVEAWAY means that we pay for *everything!* We'll even cover the shipping, and no purchase is necessary, now or later. So please return your survey today. You'll get **Two Free Books** and **Two Mystery Gifts** from each series to try, altogether worth over **$20!**

Sincerely

Pam Powers

Pam Powers
For Harlequin Reader Service

Complete the survey below and return it today to receive up to 4 FREE BOOKS and FREE GIFTS guaranteed!

▼ DETACH AND MAIL CARD TODAY!

FREE BOOKS GIVEAWAY
Reader Survey

1

Do you prefer stories with happy endings?

◯ YES   ◯ NO

2

Do you share your favorite books with friends?

◯ YES   ◯ NO

3

Do you often choose to read instead of watching TV?

◯ YES   ◯ NO

YES! Please send me my Free Rewards, consisting of **2 Free Books** from each series I select and **Free Mystery Gifts**. I understand that I am under no obligation to buy anything, as explained on the back of this card.

☐ Harlequin Desire® (225/326 HDL GQZ6)
☐ Harlequin Presents® Larger-Print (176/376 HDL GQZ6)
☐ Try Both (225/326 & 176/376 HDL GQ2J)

FIRST NAME

LAST NAME

ADDRESS

APT.#

CITY

STATE/PROV.

ZIP/POSTAL CODE

EMAIL ☐ Please check this box if you would like to receive newsletters and promotional emails from Harlequin Enterprises ULC and its affiliates. You can unsubscribe anytime.

Your Privacy – Your information is being collected by Harlequin Enterprises ULC, operating as Harlequin Reader Service. For a complete summary of the information we collect, how we use this information and to whom it is disclosed, please visit our privacy notice located at https://corporate.harlequin.com/privacy-notice. From time to time we may also exchange your personal information with reputable third parties. If you wish to opt out of this sharing of your personal information, please visit www.readerservice.com/consumerschoice or call 1-800-873-8635. **Notice to California Residents** – Under California law, you have specific rights to control and access your data. For more information on these rights and how to exercise them, visit https://corporate.harlequin.com/california-privacy.

© 2020 HARLEQUIN ENTERPRISES ULC ® and ™ are trademarks owned and used by the trademark owner and/or its licensee. Printed in the U.S.A.

HD/HP-520-FBG21

⬧ HARLEQUIN® Reader Service —Here's how it works:

Accepting your 2 free books and 2 free gifts (gifts valued at approximately $10.00 retail) places you under no obligation to buy anything. You may keep the books and gifts and return the shipping statement marked "cancel." If you do not cancel, approximately one month later we'll send you more books from the series you have chosen, and bill you at our low, subscribers-only discount price. Harlequin Presents® Larger-Print books consist of 6 books each month and cost $5.80 each in the U.S. or $5.99 each in Canada, a savings of at least 11% off the cover price. Harlequin Desire® books consist of 6 books each month and cost just $4.55 each in the U.S. or $5.24 each in Canada, a savings of at least 13% off the cover price. It's quite a bargain! Shipping and handling is just 50¢ per book in the U.S. and $1.25 per book in Canada*. You may return any shipment at our expense and cancel at any time — or you may continue to receive monthly shipments at our low, subscribers-only discount price plus shipping and handling. *Terms and prices subject to change without notice. Prices do not include sales taxes which will be charged (if applicable) based on your state or country of residence. Canadian residents will be charged applicable taxes. Offer not valid in Quebec. Books received may not be as shown. All orders subject to approval. Credit or debit balances in a customer's account(s) may be offset by any other outstanding balance owed by or to the customer. Please allow 3 to 4 weeks for delivery. Offer available while quantities last. **Your Privacy** – Your information is being collected by Harlequin Enterprises ULC, operating as Harlequin Reader Service. For a complete summary of the information we collect, how we use this information and to whom it is disclosed, please visit our privacy notice located at https://corporate.harlequin.com/privacy-notice. From time to time we may also exchange your personal information with reputable third parties. If you wish to opt out of this sharing of your personal information, please visit www.readerservice.com/consumerschoice or call 1-800-873-8635. **Notice to California Residents** – Under California law, you have specific rights to control and access your data. For more information on these rights and how to exercise them, visit https://corporate.harlequin.com/california-privacy.

▲ If offer card is missing write to: Harlequin Reader Service, P.O. Box 1341, Buffalo, NY 14240-8531 or visit www.ReaderService.com ▲

BUSINESS REPLY MAIL
FIRST-CLASS MAIL   PERMIT NO. 717   BUFFALO, NY

POSTAGE WILL BE PAID BY ADDRESSEE

HARLEQUIN READER SERVICE
PO BOX 1341
BUFFALO NY 14240-8571

NO POSTAGE
NECESSARY
IF MAILED
IN THE
UNITED STATES

And yet it was as undeniable as the sun in the sky.

She turned her face to the window as the truth hammered into her, not wanting Amelie to see her expression, knowing her face was likely drained and whitened in shock.

I love him. I love him and I can't stop it, or turn it off, or make it unhappen. I love him and it is unbearable that I do. Unbearable to love a man who pushed me from him—sent me away.

Yet bear it she must—what else could she do?

One thing only.

She set her face, still likely white as bone, knowing that all she could do now was endure and return again to being the person she had been all along. She would retreat into her safe place, where she would keep herself safe from more rejection— retreat into her familiar, self-effacing invisibility.

Evandro stood, his eyes half-lidded, before the unlit fire in the gilded salon that was seldom opened except when there was company.

As there was now.

The dozen or so guests he'd brought back with him from Turin filled the room, chattering and loud, knocking back his champagne with music blaring. The French doors were open wide to the terrace beyond, which was lit up like a stage. Several couples were out there now, dancing to the throbbing music that pulsed throughout the house and across the gardens.

'*Tesoro—mio caro!* Don't stand there like a grand *seigneur* of old. Come and dance!'

The woman gliding up to him, champagne glass in hand, her tight dress emphasising every lush curve, was well-known to him—if physical intimacy counted as knowing someone well.

Sometimes one can know a person well when a harmony exists between them that has nothing to do with how long one has known them...

He pushed the thought from his mind. It served no purpose except to reinforce why he was doing what he was doing now—filling the *palazzo* with people he didn't like and didn't care about in order to set a distance—a vital, essential distance—between himself and the person he did care about.

To protect her from me—and me from her.

As it had when he'd raced back to Turin, a sense of mocking irony assailed him at the thought that he should need such protection. The kind of protection that the woman currently inviting him into her arms could provide.

Bianca Ingrani was safe specifically because he didn't desire her. Unlike...

His eyes searched the room and found their target.

She was sitting on a chair, right at the back of the room, knees pressed together, hands folded in her lap. Her eyes were on Amelie who, overexcited by all the partying going on, was whirling around to the music, applauded by some of the guests who were making a fuss of her.

He frowned with displeasure at the outfit his daughter was wearing—another of her mother's dire choices. How had the child been allowed to don such execrable clothes tonight?

His condemning gaze went to the person who had permitted it. Her face was still—as still as the rest of her.

Invisible. She's gone invisible again.

His mouth twisted.

And can I blame her?

The question was as rhetorical as it was mocking—and the target was still himself. Always himself.

The woman he had once passed his nights with during his celebratory indulgences post-divorce followed the direction of his glance. Her expression changed.

'Who on earth is that?' Bianca exclaimed. Then her eyes went to Amelie. 'Oh, some kind of nanny… I see,' she said dismissively. Her voice turned saccharine, like sticky honey. 'How adorable your little daughter is, Evandro. I so want to meet her. Just in case…' she threw a heavily flirtatious look at her former lover '…I ever get to be her step-*mamma*.'

He watched with cynical eyes as Bianca went up to Amelie, cooing over her. While she did so, his eyes went to Jenna.

He said her name. Low, inaudible to all. Yet her eyes, which had been fixed on Amelie, then on Bianca, turned to his. But though they were open, they were closed.

Closed to him.

Closed to him for ever.

As they must be. I can allow nothing else.

He went on looking at her, his face as closed as her gaze. She sat only a handful of metres away from him, and yet she was on the other side of the world.

A cry pierced the noise around him and he turned. It had not been a cry of pain, or distress—only one of anger.

'You clumsy thing! My dress! You knocked right into me with your idiotic whirling.'

His eyes shot round to see a champagne glass rolling on the floor, its contents splashed across Bianca's tight ivory silk dress. Amelie was standing stricken, her face as white as Bianca's dress and puckering with tears. He started to move, but someone else was there before him, swooping down on Amelie, taking her hand, holding it fast.

'It's way past bedtime, poppet. You're so tired you're wobbly!'

He saw Jenna look at Bianca, whose over-made-up face still flashed with fury, all coy pretence of Amelie being 'adorable' gone.

'I do apologise,' he heard Jenna tell the other woman, her voice low and tight. 'I should have been keeping an eye on Amelie. I hope your dress can be cleaned. Amelie—come along.'

He watched her take the little girl off, out of the room. Though he had stood so close, she had not looked at him.

As if she could not bear to.

* * *

Jenna lay staring at the ceiling in her bedroom. Midnight had come and gone, and she could still hear the clash of laughter and conversation, the bass throb of the music. It was coming through the floorboards, throbbing into her head, into her misery.

The misery of seeing him again—the man she had so stupidly fallen in love with.

She had watched him roar up to the *palazzo* that afternoon in that gleaming monster car of his, followed by a cavalcade of cars and limos that had disgorged guests like birds of paradise, gorgeous in their couture clothes, their designer sunglasses, their glamour and their glitz. Talking and laughing with abandon, like noisy parakeets, they had streamed into the *palazzo*, taking it over.

And Evandro, the *seigneur*, the millionaire... billionaire? Who knew what he was, besides a member of an elite world that she was not part of and never could be?

She screwed her face up, flinching at the way she had thought herself lovely in his eyes when she'd worn that green dress, how she had glowed, thinking about his likening her to a woodland sprite...

When all along she had still been invisible. As invisible as she had been this evening, sitting there in her corner, unnoticed and ignored.

How could I possibly compare to that stunningly beautiful woman who was all over him?

She felt her heart harden. However stunningly beautiful she was, she'd upset Amelie horribly with her sudden anger. Amelie had been tearful as Jenna had hurried her upstairs, as she'd got her out of that frightful outfit she'd so wanted to wear. And Jenna had had to listen to her anguished whispers as she'd got the overtired, upset little girl into her nightgown.

'I spilt Maman's wine, once…and it was red wine…and it stained her dress…and she was so angry with me…just like that lady.' The little face had puckered again, tears welling. 'I don't like that lady—I don't! *I don't!*'

Jenna had hugged her, aching for her—and for herself. 'No one likes that lady, poppet,' she'd said. 'She's a horrid lady.'

She'd pulled Amelie's nightie over her head, guiding her towards her bed.

'Papà likes her,' Amelie had said, climbing in and looking up at Jenna, her face still anxious.

Jenna had smoothed back her hair, tucked her in, turned down her bedside light so that it only gave a glow, and stayed until sleep had taken the overwrought child. Then she'd gone back to her own room on leaden feet, hearing Amelie's parting words tolling in her brain.

'Papà likes her.'

She heard those words again, and then heard, like a bleak counterpoint against it, her own word—the single word that repeated over and over again in her head.

Fool.

Because what other word could describe her but

that? She who had never been good enough for anyone at all…

Least of all the man she had fallen in love with.

Evandro slid open the sash window of his bedroom. At last, the blessed hush of the night lapped
all around him, that infernal music silenced. There
was only the soft, incessant murmur of the cicadas—
the eternal chorus of the Mediterranean night, lifted
to the heavens. The same silver moon that had lit
the night when he had taken the woman he must not
desire into his arms hung over the deserted, darkened terrace and gardens, but it was waning now.

He knew he must not take Jenna in his arms
again. However much he ached to do so.

In his head tolled the ever-present warning his
lawyer had given him.

He sliced the window shut, knowing that what
he should do now was go to Bianca—all too willing
and waiting for him.

*If I spend the night with her—resume my affair
with her—that will put what I cannot have, dare not
have, behind me for ever.*

But revulsion filled him at the thought of Bianca's
lush embrace. She was not the woman he wanted.

Bleak-faced he retreated to his solitary bed to
stare at the ceiling, knowing sleep would elude
him, wanting what he could not have and must
not want.

Seeking the strength to stop. Failing.

* * *

For two long, endless days Jenna watched and endured. Doors opened and closed ceaselessly, and voices—overloud and piercing—filled the *palazzo*. She heard cars come and go, engines roaring, gravel scattering under tyres, music playing inside and out, heels clattering on the marble stairs and floors.

The staff were being kept on their toes, bringing food and wine and champagne, fetching and carrying. And over all the noise, cutting through it like a scimitar, were the deep tones of the man she had been such a fool over.

She tried to ignore it all—to focus only on keeping Amelie undistracted by the house parties going on all around them. After all, she reminded herself with bitter self-recrimination, Amelie was her pupil and the sole reason for her presence here. She must never forget that.

As I did so fatally that night.

Mortification burned in her. How had she thought that a man like Evandro Rocceforte might look twice at her when he had sultry beauties like Bianca Ingrani to bewitch him?

But surely he would never think of marrying her? Not when he saw how harsh she was to Amelie?

That was her sole comfort. After the incident with Bianca, Amelie did not want to join in any more with all that was going on downstairs, so Jenna did not have to witness Evandro and Bianca together.

Except in her tormented imagination.

There, it was impossible, in her misery, to banish images of them together…

Evandro stood out on the gravelled carriage sweep, watching the last of the motorcade heading off. Relief filled him. They were gone, the whole damn crowd of them. Taking Bianca with them and leaving him with one resolve. A resolve that had formed and then hardened with every moment since their arrival.

I brought them here—brought Bianca here—with one purpose only: to sever myself from the woman I must not desire.

But the attempt had been useless, instead serving only to have the opposite effect.

In his mind's eye he saw Jenna again, sitting there in the salon like a ghost…lost to him.

But I will not lose her. I will not. I refuse to turn away from her.

His benighted marriage had ruined enough of his life. For this, for what was happening now, he wished Berenice and all her lawyers to hell, despite her threats.

I'll seize what happiness I can while I can. Cost me what it may—I'll pay the price.

Resolve strengthening, he strode indoors with only one destination in mind.

He vaulted the stairs as if the devil himself were goading him on—and laughing as he did so.

But he did not care for devils—nor their mocking laughter.

CHAPTER NINE

'AMELIE, YOU STILL have another page of sums. They won't go away until you've done them.'

Jenna's voice was sympathetic, but firm. Like Amelie, she'd heard the noise of the departing house party—the loud goodbyes and the cars disappearing into the distance—but now it had gone quiet.

'Can I not go and find my *papà* now?' Amelie asked plaintively. 'Now that all the people have gone?'

'He'll ask for you or come and see you when he's ready,' Jenna replied, and her reluctant pupil sighed.

Then suddenly she sat up straight, turning her head towards the schoolroom door. Footsteps, rapid and distinctive, sounded outside on the landing.

'Papà!' cried Amelie, ecstatic.

Jenna had only a second to prepare. To steel herself. Then the door was flying open and Evandro was striding in.

Amelie launched herself at him and he caught her up, swinging her around in a bear hug, then put her back on her feet.

'Time for a swim,' he said. 'Be off and get your things.'

Amelie needed no urging, and hurtled happily out of the room.

Evandro straightened, heading straight for Jenna with purpose in his stride, gold glinting in his slate eyes. Catching her face in his hands, he turned it up to him. And then he crushed her mouth with his.

'Who's for ice cream?' Evandro's question rang out over the swimming pool.

'Me! Me!'

Amelie scrambled out of the water, running up to him where he stood, three towering cornets clustered in his hand, freshly scooped from the freezer in the kitchens. Happily seizing the one he offered her, she settled down on a sun lounger to consume it.

'That just leaves us,' he said, lowering himself down on the lounger beside Jenna and handing her one of the two cones he still held.

She took it, knowing her eyes were glowing. She had felt as if she were glowing—as if the sun itself was radiating from inside her—since Evandro had swept her up into that crushing, possessing kiss.

Dear God, could it really be true? Had it really happened? Had she gone, in a single moment, from misery and anguish and hopelessness to radiant happiness?

But it had happened, and it was true—entirely true!

His kiss had been everything she could have dreamt of. And as he'd released her he'd cupped her cheek with his hand. Pooled his gold-shot gaze with hers.

'Forgive me,' he'd said.

And in that instant, in that moment, it had been all that needed to be said. The rest of his apology had been in his eyes, in the clasp of her hand in his, in the smile playing at his mouth, as it did now, as he watched her catch at the fast-melting ice-cream.

She asked for no more. No more than this. This happiness so profound that it was in every pore of her being, every cell in her body. She did not question it or examine it—only accepted it. With all her heart.

Evandro leant back against the trunk of the ancient chestnut tree that edged the woods above the *palazzo* gardens. The afternoon had become close and sultry, so they had brought a picnic high tea up here to the woods, where there was more shade from the oppressive heat. A little way away Amelie was playing teddy bears' picnic, with leaves for plates and acorns for cups, absorbed in her game.

He was glad of it—it allowed him to give more attention to Jenna.

He drew her back against him, leaving the remains of their picnic on the rug.

'She's happy,' Jenna said, looking across to Amelie.

There was a warmth in her voice, a fondness, that made it sweet for him.

'And so am I,' he said, nestling her under his shoulder. 'Totally and entirely happy.'

Because happiness was what he was going to claim. The happiness he had never thought would come his way. The happiness that had been bestowed upon him by this special woman—his very own woodland sprite…as he had called her from the first.

He smiled to think of it, their first encounter that had started him on this path and led him here, to this. This happiness he was claiming now. A summer's happiness…that nothing, surely, could blight…

From far away, through the too-still haze, across the heat-pooled valley where the hot gold sunshine was slowly turning to molten bronze, came a low, scarcely audible tremor on the windless air.

Amelie's fair head lifted from where she was playing. 'What was that, Papà?' A thread of anxiety was in her voice.

'Thunder,' he said. 'This heat must break, so a storm is coming.' His eyes went upward, beyond the leafy bower under which they sat. Clouds were massing, and he could feel the static building in the atmosphere.

'Are you sure it's going to be a storm?' Jenna sat up, looking out over the vista.

Amelie clambered to her feet. 'I don't like storms,' she said fearfully.

Jenna got up as well. 'Evandro, perhaps we'd better go back. Woods are not the safest places in a thunderstorm.'

She started to close up the picnic basket, and Evandro levered himself to his feet.

'It may pass by,' he said. 'The storm may never break—'

But Amelie was already setting off, teddy bears clutched to her chest, and Jenna was following with rug and cushions, leaving him the picnic basket. The sky was darkening overhead now, the static mounting, and the bronze sun had disappeared behind heavy clouds.

He hurried them all back to the *palazzo*, welcoming the failing daylight, whatever the cause. After all, when night came it would, he knew, bring him his heart's desire…

Night meshed them in, and the airless stillness of the dark embraced them as they embraced each other. Evandro's strong body arched over hers and it was wonderful to her…wondrous that he desired her, was claiming her as he was now.

Joy filled her and she pulled his mouth to hers, feeling the arousing pleasure of his deepening kiss. And it was a pleasure that was only beginning, that grew more and yet more as his hand gently but insistently slid between her thighs, which slackened to his caressing touch. His other hand moved between her breasts, his skilled fingers ministering to them so that wave after wave of a pleasure she had never tasted before brought little sighs and catches from her throat.

His mouth lifted from hers, descending to one breast and then the other in turn, engendering yet more catches in her throat and then, quite distinctly,

a moan of pleasure so exquisite her eyes could only
flutter shut with it as his hand, parting her thighs,
found what it was seeking with infinite skill and
slow, sure movements.

She knew, with an uplifting of her heart, that he
was making her ready for him. Her moans came
again, her spine arching now, hands spearing into
the nape of his strong neck as his dark head lowered
to her ripened breasts.

And then, as her pleasure mounted and mounted
more, and a restlessness started to fill her, making
her legs strain outwards, it was as if her body, driven
by an instinct older than time itself, was readying
itself to receive him.

He was lifting his head from her breasts, kissing her mouth once more, before easing his long,
powerful body so that with a movement so smooth
she did not realise it was about to happen he sought
his way within her. His control was absolute—she
knew that—and she knew it was for her sake that
he was bending every fibre of his will to make this
moment the way it should be…a wondrous union of
flesh with flesh.

And she took him into her, holding him, cradling
him within her body, within the circle of her arms.

He lay still for a little while, as her body accom-
modated itself to his, before slowly, infinitely slowly,
and infinitely arousingly, he started to move within
her. He stroked her hair and his hand, she realised,
was trembling very slightly as he took his weight on
his arm, not wanting, she knew, to crush her.

Then, his eyes holding hers in the dim light of the night, he lowered his mouth to kiss her softly, exquisitely. Once more she felt as if a glow were starting up inside her—a warmth, a heat, a pleasure so extraordinary, so intense, welling up and melting through her. It was a pleasure she had never known nor imagined, consuming her whole body, her whole being. Wonder filled her, lifted her spine, parted her lips...

And it went on and on, flowing through her to every extremity of her body, this molten fusion of her being combined with his.

With the dimmest part of her consciousness she realised that he was moving faster within her, that his torso was lifting from her, his muscled thighs straining now against hers, his body rearing up, head thrown back. She felt their bodies meld into each other, fusing in the heat that was making them one single, searing flesh.

Did she cry out? She didn't know—knew only that it was the most glorious moment of her life, and that she was giving, and had been given, a gift whose worth was infinite.

Love poured from her—and if it was a love he'd never asked for, never sought, it did not matter. Because it was her gift, freely given, in return for this burning moment of union, of ecstatic joy.

His arms enfolded her and she felt the sheen of his exhaustion on his cooling skin. She knew it was the same for her as he drew her close into his encircling embrace. She felt his breath, warm and ragged, at her shoulder.

'Did I hurt you? For all the world I would not have—'

She heard the tremor in his low voice and caught his hand, curving it into hers, turning and lifting her head so it was resting against his broad chest, allowing her to brush his lips with reassurance.

'You will never hurt me,' she said.

And in her eyes, though it was too dark for him to see, was all the love she had for him and always would.

It was in the early hours of the morning that the storm rolled in, with thunderous clouds unleashing a torrent of rain upon the *palazzo* and lightning jagging the night. The tempest was silent at first, felt only through the charged static of the atmosphere, then it was ripping through the sky with a belligerent crackling roar of deafening thunder and noise.

Evandro levered himself up from the bed and strode to the window to lower the sash, shutting it against the driving rain exploding out of the heavens, pounding down upon the stone paving of the terrace below like bullets as another fork of lightning sliced across the sky and another thunderclap crashed overhead.

'Amelie!'

Jenna's anxious voice made him turn. 'I'll go to her.'

He seized his bathrobe, belting it swiftly around him, and left the room, returning moments later.

'Sound asleep,' he announced.

He discarded his robe, getting back into bed and wrapping Jenna in his arms. It was all that he wanted.

Certainty filled him. And defiance too.

He had made his declaration—claimed Jenna for his own. This woman who was everything that Berenice was not, nor ever could be with her cankered soul. Jenna—whose clear-seeing eyes, kindness and compassion, honesty and sincerity, quiet ways and subtle beauty, could wash away the taint of his accursed marriage and draw from him all its poison.

He would not turn away from her again.

He did not care—*would* not care.

If there was danger, so be it.

If there was risk, he would face it.

But until they came—*if* they came—he would have all the happiness that surely life owed him after so many bitter, wasted years.

All the happiness that the woman in his arms could gift him.

Jenna—his sweet Jenna—his own, his blessing and his bounty.

He folded her to him, feeling her soft, warm body moulding to his, hearing her gentle breathing easing into sleep once more.

The storm started to die away as swiftly as it had broken, thunder descending to a mere rumbling, lightning to mere flickers. His arms tightened around her, holding her close, so close.

It was the only place he wanted her to be.

With him.

His breathing slowed, his limbs becoming heavy, and sleep washed over him…with Jenna safe in his arms.

Outside, jagging down from the fleeing storm clouds, a fork of lightning more vivid than anything before illuminated the woodland above the gardens in lurid, livid light.

But the crack of thunder that came an instant later was not the only deafening sound to be heard.

At the edge of the woods the chestnut tree Evandro and Jenna had sat under only a few hours ago split violently in two, severed by the final vicious knifing of the storm.

CHAPTER TEN

'WELL, IT WILL save on the watering,' Evandro said cheerfully, surveying the rain-battered gardens.

His eyes went to Jenna, bathing her in a visual caress, and the sight of her standing next to Amelie out on the still-damp terrace, where the bright, clear morning air was sparkling and fresh, lifted his heart.

I have them both—Jenna and Amelie. All that I could ever want.

'The world new-made,' he heard her say now, a smile at her lips.

The world new-made.

Her words echoed inside him, resonating with a clarity and an intensity that crystallised all that he felt.

I have made it new—made the world new for myself...

Clean and clear and untainted by the world he had lived in with Berenice.

But he would not remember her or think of her. The long shadow she had cast over his life, blighting it, must never reach here...not now.

He shook his head free of the thought, placing his arm around Jenna's slender shoulders, drawing her against him and dropping a kiss upon her head. Then, taking Amelie's hand in his, he held it tight in a silent vow never to let it go.

They were his. The woman he had claimed as his and the child he would always protect and cherish.

For an instant, as the vow formed so vehemently in his head, he saw a shadow pass across the face of the bright sun. Heard—as if in an ugly echo, summoned by his unwelcome thought of Berenice— her mocking, vengeful laugh…

He banished it.

He squeezed Jenna's shoulder, and Amelie's hand.

'So, what shall we do this wonderful day?' he asked genially, his heart glowing within him. 'Shall we have another pool day, or drive off somewhere? And, if so, where? And if we stay here, shall we have another tea party and dress up in our best again? Or have a dinner party, and even more dressing up?'

Amelie caught on the last option he'd suggested. 'Dressing up!' she cried enthusiastically. 'Oh, Papà, can we dress up like Miss Jenna said? Like the children at her school did?'

He smiled down at her. 'Why not?' He nodded. 'Will you be the silver fairy you described?' Then his eyes went to Jenna, softening. 'Though that should be you—*you* are the good fairy in my life.' His eyes held hers. 'Breaking the evil spell…'

Her hand lifted to his face, her eyes full of

warmth. 'And you, Evandro, are my Prince Charming,' she said.

He gave a crack of laughter, dropping a light kiss upon her mouth, then ushered them all to the breakfast table. As they settled down around it he reached for the coffee pot and another brilliant idea struck him.

'You know what I think?' he asked. 'How about taking a holiday? At the seaside? We'll go next week.'

Amelie's eyes brightened at the magic word. 'Yes…*yes*! Seaside! Seaside!' she exclaimed excitedly.

'You've done it now,' Jenna murmured, smiling. 'No going back on it now that you've said it.'

He grinned. 'I have no intention of going back on it—on anything.'

No, there would be no going back now. And nothing that might yet come would threaten his newfound, wondrous happiness.

But it might not come.

That was what he must cling to.

The same reckless defiance that had filled him as he'd sent Bianca and her friends packing—the defiance that had steeled him with ruthless resolve and sent him racing up the stairs to stride into Amelie's schoolroom and claim the woman he wanted, despite all his own warnings to himself, now filled him again.

His gaze swept between them, Jenna and Amelie. Then moved out beyond them, across the sunlit gardens to where, at the edge of the wood, the burnt and stricken chestnut, severed by that final lightning bolt, lurched brokenly, blackened and crippled.

Victim of the storm that had broken overhead, destroying all that defied it.

'This is bliss!'

Jenna leant back, legs outstretched, on the warm, soft sand, her arms straight behind her, her palms supporting her weight. Her hair was held back by a colourful bandeau and she lifted her face to the sun.

But then, all of life was bliss these days. How could it be anything else?

Her eyes went to Evandro, lounging on the sand beside her, and her insides gave a little flip. Evandro in a business suit was powerful and formidable. Evandro in chinos, an open-necked shirt and deck shoes was darkly, magnetically attractive. But Evandro lying as he was now, on his side, a hand supporting his head, his magnificent body completely on show apart from the bathing shorts he was wearing, was simply…breathtaking.

'You look like a fifties film star,' he was saying now, his eyes lazily appreciative. 'But twice as glamorous.'

His eyes held hers, and in them was a look that made Jenna wish they were not on the private beach at this extremely swish family resort in the Cinque Terre, but in their own bedroom.

To deflect her thoughts, she looked towards the sea's edge, where Amelie was playing with another little girl she'd palled up with. They were busy building a sandcastle together.

'It's so wonderful to see Amelie so happy,' she said warmly. Her eyes went back to Evandro and that warmth was still in them. Her gaze softened even more. 'You are a *wonderful* father, Evandro—you would do anything for her.'

There was a catch in her voice as she spoke. She was remembering her own father, who had done nothing for her—never loved or wanted her, only ignored and resented her. She dropped her eyes, not wanting to remember.

And then Amelie was running up to them, asking if she and Luisa could go and get ice creams from the beach bistro.

'If Luisa is allowed by her parents,' said Evandro, and the two children hared off to where Luisa's parents, with a smaller toddler in tow, were sitting on sun loungers in the shade of a parasol.

The mother nodded at her daughter's request, smiling across at Jenna and Evandro as the girls ran off to the bistro.

'You two have a lovely little daughter,' the woman called across to them. 'With excellent manners!'

'I return the compliment entirely,' Evandro assured her.

Jenna saw the other woman's eyes linger a moment on Evandro and could not begrudge her—because his physique *was* perfect. Powerful and smoothly muscled, long-legged and...

She ran out of adjectives, but knew she did not

need them. She had the real thing, so words just weren't important.

There were other words that lingered in her head instead.

'You two have a lovely little daughter.'

They echoed again now, and with them came the memory of how she'd stood out on the terrace at the *palazzo*, watching the sun set with Amelie and Evandro.

Like a family...

Emotion welled in her. It had not been true then, and she'd berated herself for the thought.

But are we now...a family?

If wishing could make it so, then it would be true. But though she might love Evandro, and though he might desire her—wonderful as it was that he did— was that enough to make her dream come true?

And is it his dream?

The question lingered in her head like a crab pincering its claws on her flesh. And for all the happiness and joy that flooded her day after golden day, night after passionate night, it lingered still.

Unanswered.

Unanswerable.

After their fortnight at the seaside—leisurely days on the beach interspersed with days exploring the charm and delights of the famed Cinque Terre, visiting the impossibly pretty harbour villages with their painted houses climbing up steep cliffs, lunching at open-air trattorias, taking boat trips out to sea to spot dolphins and flying fish—Evandro announced that he could no longer postpone looking in at his office.

So they drove north, inland to Turin, after Amelie and Luisa had vowed faithfully to message each other daily, as proof of their enduring friendship.

In Turin, Jenna settled down with Amelie in Evandro's ferociously modernistic apartment, using the time he was at work to resume her pupil's studies. Evandro pitched in as well, helping his daughter with maths every evening upon his return from the office.

'Imagine if I couldn't do my sums correctly,' he quizzed Amelie. 'I wouldn't be able to tell if I was making any money at all—or, far worse, if the bridges and dams Rocceforte Industriale builds would fall down!'

'You're so good with her,' Jenna said to him fondly, when the maths book had finally been put away and Amelie had been released to play her favourite computer game online with Luisa before dinner. 'A natural-born father. It's clearly in the genes.'

She kissed him lightly on the cheek, wanting him to be free of the doubts he'd once had that he could be a good father after so much separation from his daughter.

But he did not reply—only got to his feet, his expression suddenly shuttered.

A moment later it was gone, replaced with a smile.

'So, what gastronomical delights are in store

for tonight?' he asked, and there was only good-humoured enquiry in his face.

'I thought I might do something completely different,' Jenna answered solemnly and straight-faced, knowing the limit of her culinary skills. 'Pasta in a totally different shape from last night's.'

He laughed, strolling into the kitchen to the huge fridge to fetch himself a beer and settling down at the breakfast bar to oversee the preparation of the sauce she would painstakingly assemble from vegetables freshly purchased that morning.

It was a pleasure to venture out with Amelie—not just to explore the busy, bustling city together, with its mix of architectural styles, boulevards and covered arcades, but for the fun of feeling like an Italian housewife doing the daily shop—confirming to her, if she needed confirmation, that all her joy stemmed from being with Evandro and his daughter, enjoying these ordinary, domestic days.

Like a family.

As she added freshly chopped beef tomatoes to the sauce and stirred them in, the ache for it to be so for ever rose piercingly within her. Perhaps one day he would love her as she loved him...

And one day he will see a future that has me in it—a happy future for him and Amelie, after all the misery his marriage put him through.

But would it come, that day? *Could* it come?

The sound of Evandro's phone ringing was an interruption she welcomed to thoughts that were as fruitless as they were aching.

* * *

Evandro lifted his phone from the breakfast bar, expecting it to be the project manager he'd asked to report in that evening. But the call was from someone quite different.

'Evandro, *cara*, my spies tell me you are back in town!'

The sultry tones were breathed across the ether, and he gave a silent curse that he had not checked the caller before answering.

'Bianca,' he replied evenly, keeping his voice neutral. He was aware that Jenna had stopped stirring the fragrant contents of the saucepan and had half turned, before freezing.

'You must have been bored out of your mind in the country once we'd all gone,' Bianca was purring now. 'Come over for drinks—and anything else you might feel like…' She trailed off seductively.

'That isn't going to be possible,' he said.

He kept his tone somewhere between even and repressive. He'd prefer, if he could, to get out of this gracefully. He caught at the one thing he could say to put Bianca off—other than the truth. Which was none of her damn business.

No one's business except mine and Jenna's.

The defiance with which he'd claimed the happiness he was now enjoying with Jenna filled him again. As for Bianca Ingrani—she was swiftly dismissible.

'I've got Amelie with me,' he told her.

Bianca's annoyance was obvious. 'What a shame,'

she said. 'Of course, there are always agency nannies who can be summoned to babysit,' she said hopefully.

'Thank you—but I already have someone. The woman you took to be Amelie's nanny—Jenna,' he heard himself reply. Then cursed himself.

Accidenti. Why had he given anything away to the likes of Bianca Ingrani?

'Jenna?' Suspicion twisted in Bianca's voice at his casual use of her forename. 'You brought that girl to your *apartment*?'

And suddenly, impatiently, Evandro was fed up with it—with Bianca's persistence in trying to renew their affair. He wanted to get rid of her in the quickest way possible, even if it was none of her business.

'Yes,' he said tightly, 'Jenna is with me here.' He took a breath, urging her to get the message. 'Bianca, I'm sorry if you had hopes we might get back together again, but that isn't possible. I've moved on.' He made his voice conciliatory, complimentary, for courtesy's sake. 'Our time together was good, and I wish you all the very best—and a better man for you than me.'

He rang off, wanting only to be done with her. He turned back to Jenna, who was stirring the sauce again, but with jerky, mechanical motions. He set down his phone before winding his arms around her waist from behind, nuzzling her neck.

'Relax,' he said. 'I've given Bianca her marching orders.' He drew her close and felt her lean back against him, her muscles relaxing.

'She's so incredibly beautiful,' he heard her say, a little wistfully.

'Not to me—not any more,' he replied. 'And besides…' his voice hardened '…do you seriously imagine I would want to have anything to do with a woman who could speak as angrily as she did to Amelie at the *palazzo*? Upsetting her the way she did? No,' he finished decisively, 'Bianca is over and done with. She's nothing to me now.'

He turned Jenna around to him, not wanting her worrying a second longer about Bianca Ingrani, kissing her lightly at first, then more deeply, feeling passion build. But reluctantly he relinquished her. Now was not the moment—especially when Amelie's voice piped up from the doorway.

'Is dinner ready? Can I grate the cheese? Luisa and I were searching for unicorns—she found one and I found two!'

She babbled on happily, fetching parmesan from the huge fridge and sitting herself on one of the tall stools at the breakfast bar to start grating. Evandro reached for his half-consumed beer and fetched a bottle of chilled white wine from the wine fridge, pouring glasses for Jenna and himself as she put the fresh pasta on to cook.

An everyday, cosy, domestic scene…the three of them at dinner, convivial, affectionate and united.

What I never had with Berenice.

Once, at the start of his marriage, he had thought—hoped—that it might be so. Before those futile hopes had been destroyed.

His ex had destroyed everything—everything she had power over.

His eyes rested now on Amelie, busy with her grating, and then on Jenna, still at the stove. A chill plucked at him.

What else will she seek to destroy, that woman who cursed my life?

But he knew—he knew just what she would want to destroy next.

If she ever found out…

CHAPTER ELEVEN

THE *PALAZZO* WAS warm and welcoming when they returned a fortnight later. Evandro had interspersed his work with showing Jenna and Amelie the sights of the region, from the rich Piedmontese countryside surrounding Turin to the splendours of the Alpine lakes and mountains beyond, making a second holiday of it.

Signora Farrafacci was welcoming, too, and all the other staff.

Amelie ran upstairs with Loretta and Maria to show them her holiday souvenirs and give them the presents she'd bought for them—a carved wooden donkcy each from the seaside, and a stylish scarf from a very upmarket fashion house in Turin.

The scarves had not been the only items purchased there—Evandro had indulged Amelie in some judiciously selected frills and Jenna, too, had been the recipient of his indulgence.

She had yielded to his insistence on enlarging her wardrobe with clothes she could never have afforded on her teacher's salary—even the generous one he was paying her—for two reasons only: to look her very best for him, and to see his eyes light up when she wore the beautiful outfits he'd lavished on her.

A homecoming feast awaited them on their first night back at the *palazzo*. And as she walked into the dining room with Amelie, her eyes went straight to Evandro, resplendent in a tuxedo for the occasion. Jenna felt a flush of pleasure go through her as his eyes swept over her, knowing that the beautiful evening gown she was wearing—dusky pink, cut on the bias—did things for her slender figure that were only and entirely for his benefit.

He kissed her hand with bowing gallantry. *'Bellissima,'* he murmured, his voice husky, his eyes speaking volumes. Then, tearing his gaze away, he dropped it to Amelie. 'And you, too, *carina*!' he exclaimed, and made a performance of kissing Amelie's hand as well, with smacking kisses which made her giggle.

Amelie's dress was pink, too, but pale as a rosebud, with a little bolero jacket.

'Which of us is prettier, Papà?' Amelie's voice piped up. 'You have to choose between us!'

Jenna glanced at Evandro, expecting him to make some jocular remark about the impossibility of his daughter's demand. But it did not come. Instead there was something in his face, just for a fleeting second, that made her suddenly go still.

It lasted only a moment, making her think she had imagined it, and then he was turning to fill their glasses with champagne and highly diluted Buck's Fizz for Amelie.

'To coming home!' he proclaimed.

The word *home*—so simple, so powerful—resonated in Jenna's head.

Let this be home—oh, sweet heaven, let this be home.

Home for ever, with the little girl she had come to love and the man she always would…

Longing filled her hope-filled heart. A heart that would surely break if she hoped in vain.

Evandro hung up the phone with satisfaction. He'd just booked Amelie into the summer holiday camp run by the convent school where she would be starting in the autumn. It would do her good to meet some of her future fellow pupils, as well as enjoy all the activities provided at the camp.

He had another motive for sending her too—a much more selfish motive. It would give him undivided access to Jenna. He would still have to pay attention to his work, of course—his responsibilities were too great to ignore—but other than that… He found himself wanting to take advantage of all the time he had left with her.

With sudden restlessness, he got to his feet. Though it was good—*very* good—to be back at the *palazzo*, he felt an impulse, powerful and compelling, to set off again. Somewhere far away, remote… Australia, New Zealand, the South Seas, even.

Just the three of us—Amelie, Jenna and me.
Somewhere far, far away, beyond the reach of—

A light tap at the library door made him start. It was his housekeeper, coming in with his usual mid-morning coffee.

'Thank you.' He made himself smile, wanting his unwelcome thoughts banished.

He took the tray from her to deposit it on his desk and resumed his chair, but she did not leave.

'Is there something else, Signora Farrafacci?' he enquired courteously. There seemed to be an air of expectation about her, and her smile was fulsome.

'I just want to say,' she opened, 'how very much I—and all the staff—hope that for once all those pesky paparazzi are right. *We* would certainly welcome it!'

Evandro frowned. 'Paparazzi?' he said blankly.

'Normally, of course,' his housekeeper continued, 'I ignore all those rubbishy articles.' She gave a dismissive sniff. 'But in this case… Well…' her expression softened '…*such* a nice young lady, Signorina Jenna, and a *much* better choice to be the Signora Rocceforte you *deserve* after all you've been through—and poor little Amelie.' She drew breath, nodding. 'I've said quite enough for now—I'll leave you to your work.'

She sailed out, oblivious to the bomb she had just exploded in her employer's face.

As she closed the door behind her Evandro felt himself very slowly unfreeze. But it was an unfreezing that was like boiling oil being poured through his veins.

After his divorce he'd become inured to the prurient interest of the tabloids as he'd celebrated his newly single freedom. Bianca, he knew, had actively fed them stories about their affair, tipping the paparazzi off as to where he and she might be hitting the nightspots in Turin, Milan and Rome, angling things so that one day she might be described not coyly as his 'constant companion' but as his *'fidenzata'*—fiancée.

His mind raced urgently. He'd known the danger he was courting in claiming Jenna for himself right from the start—known the risks. But he'd overridden them, resolving—even after all his warnings to himself—that they were worth taking for what Jenna bestowed upon him. What he so wanted.

He'd done his best to minimise those risks. All the time he, Jenna and Amelie had been away he'd been scrupulous in keeping a deliberately low profile—choosing a family seaside resort that would hardly attract the attention of any paps wanting to snap the famous and fashionable and then, in Turin, deliberately not being seen out with Jenna—that single shopping expedition aside.

So, how the hell…?

He yanked his keyboard to him, urgently searching. In moments the offending article leapt on to the screen in front of him—along with photos.

He froze all over again.

Bianca. Had she vented her anger at his dismissal

to her tame hack, who'd promptly scented a bigger story and gone digging for it?

The story claimed that Turin's most eligible *scapolo* had a new woman in his life whom he was treating with kid gloves—no louche nightspots and clubbing for them—and was already living with, having installed her in his apartment.

No way, the article purred in saccharine tones, could this unknown *signorina* be nothing more than his daughter's nanny... Not when the *vendeuse* at an exclusive fashion boutique had confirmed that he'd spent a fortune on couture clothes for her. Not when all three of them had been photographed leaving the shop, with Evandro Rocceforte's arm around the *signorina*'s shoulder, the two of them gazing at each other in *so* enamoured a fashion. Not when there were photos of the two *signorinas* going to the food market together, just like mother and daughter...

The article trilled on...

> *Can it be wedding bells in the offing, we wonder? Will it be second time lucky for newly divorced Evandro Rocceforte? A happy new family for his adorable little daughter—with a new mamma and a new love for our dashing Evandro?*
> *We hope so! How we adore a happy ending!*

Evandro stared at the screen, his blood turning to ice.

Hell. Hell and damnation!

I should have been more careful—more discreet. I should never have spoken to Bianca, never have taken Jenna to Turin...

He threw himself back in his leather chair, staring ahead with bleak, impotent fury, his hands clenched over the arms of his chair, his mind filled with grim foreboding...

And in his head tolled the warning his lawyer had given him as he'd signed those papers the other man had so reluctantly put in front of him.

'Do you realise the implications of what you are agreeing to?'

And the words his lawyer had spoken next.

'She can destroy your future.'

The iron grip of his hands tightened. Would the inevitable letter come, fulfilling his lawyer's warning? Would the storm break over his head? Or would Berenice never find out about this damnable article?

He just did not know.

Face dark, jaw steeled, he knew all he could do now was wait.

And hope.

'Don't move.'

Evandro's voice was low and intense as Jenna's naked body was illuminated only by the full moon shining through the bedroom window.

'Don't move,' he said again. 'I want you exactly... *exactly*...like this.'

He knelt over her, his powerful legs caging her, and lifted her hands over her head, where her hair streamed across the pillow. A rasp broke from him as he straightened, one hand reaching down to shape her breast, and let his thumb play idly over her cresting nipple so that it peaked and strained against his palm.

She felt her back arch, heard a moan of pleasure sound in her throat. Her eyes clung to his and Evandro's eyes did not leave hers for an instant as he lowered his other hand to the secret vee between her thighs, easing into the delicate folds.

Her moan came again, more helpless yet, and her eyes fluttered shut as she gave herself over to the unbearably exquisite sensations he was drawing from her with his skilled stroking. She felt him lean forward slightly, making her aware of just how aroused he was, and she gloried in the knowledge. She ached for his possession, but he would not let her take him yet.

She felt her response mounting, the low, helpless moans in her throat coming faster and faster, and her lips parted, her head rolling back at how exquisitely, blissfully close she was as pleasure surmounted pleasure, growing and building, seeking the release she was now desperate for. The release that only he could give her.

She felt her spine arching in supplication… And then, just as she felt she could bear no more arousal, no more delay, his hands lifted from palming her straining breasts and the aching vee between her parted thighs. He was moving now, with a sudden, decisive, surging clenching of his taut-muscled thighs around her hips. He lifted her urgently, coming over her naked, hungry body with his hard and powerful one, and thrust into her, filling her body with his.

She gave a cry, her hands flying to his shoulders, clutching at their strength as he drove into her. Her legs netted his, and she cried out again as wave after wave of a bliss—a pleasure so intense she could not bear it—broke through her, consuming her.

She felt the molten fusion of their bodies uniting them, melding them each to the other, and she cried out his name and all but sobbed as she slowly, so very slowly, descended from the indescribable peak he had taken her to.

Her trembling body was still clinging to his as he gently relinquished her, drawing her back against him, his breath ragged on her shoulder. She could feel the pounding slug of his heartbeat, beating in time with her own.

Had it ever been that intense before? Had there been an urgency—almost a desperation—and a ravening hunger in his lovemaking tonight? As if the need to possess her had possessed him?

She lay in the strong circle of his arms, felt his embrace closer, tighter, than she had known it before, as he moulded her slender body against his as if he would never, never let her go.

Gladness filled her, and a sense of blessing so great that she felt her body relax now, her hectic heart and breathing easing along with his. She murmured his name, the syllables like a sweet caress, and folded her small hand over his much larger one.

How much she loved him. How very much...

The words blurred in her mind as consciousness was clouded with the soft, cocooning blanket of sweet slumber. Uniting them both in its somnolent embrace.

They were breakfasting, as usual, out on the terrace. Amelie was chattering away, enthusiastically telling them about all the fun things she was doing at summer camp. It was her second week there, and Jenna was so glad she was enjoying it. Not just for Amelie's sake, but also for her own. Darling though Amelie was, it was wonderful to have Evandro all to herself.

Her eyes went to him now. He was drinking his coffee, and there was a distracted air about him that had, she thought, been noticeable before from time to time, in the shuttering of his face or the veiling of his eyes.

Was he remembering Berenice, and his bitter unhappiness with her?

But he was free of her now. Free to find new happiness. Free to make his life anew.

And, oh, please let it be with me.

The familiar longing lodged so deep in her heart burned in her as ever, warring with the fear that she was longing for what could never be...

He looked up as Maria sallied forth onto the terrace, informing Amelie that the car was ready to drive her to summer camp. The little girl vaulted to her feet, grabbing her kitbag and bestowing a kiss upon Jenna's cheek and a quick hug upon her father, before gaily running off.

'For you, *signor*,' Maria said to Evandro, and deposited a clutch of mail beside his plate before taking herself off again.

As he did every morning when presented with the post, he started to leaf through it immediately, purposefully—presumably looking for work-related items, Jenna assumed. Halfway through the pile, he stilled. Then, abruptly, he extracted one of the letters and got to his feet. Not looking at her.

'Excuse me.'

His voice sounded terse, and tension was visible in his stance as he strode indoors. Jenna could only stare after him. Cold pooled inside her, and suddenly she did not want any more coffee.

Something is wrong.

And all the fears she had sought to dispel came rushing back.

The heavily embossed paper lay on Evandro's desk, the ornate lettering of the name of the very expensive lawyers Berenice used leaping out at him, and the words they had written imprinted like red-hot metal on his brain.

So it had come.

The storm was breaking over him—he had not escaped it.

He took a heavy, ragged breath that seared his lungs.

Memory mocked him. Memories of that very first night at dinner, when he and Jenna had spoken of evil enchantresses and the malign spells they cast upon their victims.

'All such spells can be broken,' Jenna had told him.

Not this one.

A savage snarl broke from him and his fist crashed down upon the lawyer's letter—the letter that activated Berenice's final weapon against him. The weapon he was powerless to deflect. Powerless to defeat.

His defiance had been in vain. And now he could only do what must be done. He had no choice but to honour the vow he had made—no matter the cost.

And it *would* cost him. But not *just* him.

That was the bitterest part of all…

Jenna was in the schoolroom, sorting Amelie's schoolbooks. There were no lessons now that she was at summer camp all day, so Jenna was packing them away, putting aside the ones she herself had brought to Italy and putting the rest into a cupboard. Her mood was heavy, and that feeling that something was wrong still assailed her.

Mechanically, she went on, neatly putting Amelie's exercise books in subject order.

She heard Evandro's distinctive heavy tread out on the landing before he opened the door. And as he did, for a split second she had a flashback to the moment when Bianca and her friends had departed and he had come striding in, seizing her up, crushing her into his arms. Making her his own.

Then the memory was gone. He stood still inside the doorway, not coming forward. She paused in her actions and looked at him. His face was set, the deep lines scored around his mouth more pronounced than usual, and his expression was shuttered. Closed to her.

A sudden dread consumed her.

'Jenna.'

He said her name. Staccato, terse. He was forcing himself to say what he had to say—in the way that he must say it.

'I've heard…' he began, and the lie was forming in his head—the acceptable lie, the necessary lie. 'I've heard from my aunt. She is my father's older sister, and lives in Sorrento. She wants to meet Amelie—she's never yet had the opportunity, as she disliked Berenice and the dislike was mutual—and of course I would like Amelie to meet her great-aunt.'

He tried to make his voice sound reasonable, conversational.

But she was standing there motionless, frozen, the colour slowly leaching from her face.

She knows. She knows what I am doing.

Emotion twisted inside him, savage and cruel, sinking its fangs into his own flesh. But he forced

himself on—there was no other way. No other way
to do this.

'So, given that Amelie is now in summer camp,
and when it finishes and before term starts I shall
be taking her to Sorrento, this seems an opportune
time for you to…' He stopped. Made himself shrug
though his shoulders felt like lead, crushing his
lungs. 'It's been good, this summer with you,' he
said. 'And I shall remember it with appreciation.
But—' He stopped again.

She was looking at him, but it was in the way
she'd looked at him when he'd brought Bianca here,
when Jenna had sat as white-faced as she was now.
As if she was looking at him not just across the
schoolroom, but across the space that parted them…
the space that they could now never cross.

'You've moved on,' she said.

There was nothing in her voice—nothing at all.
Nothing in her eyes or her face.

They were the words he'd said to get Bianca out of
his life. He nodded. It took all his strength to do so.

Something changed in her face and she began to
speak again. At first he did not hear her. Then he did.

'When would you like me to leave?'

He did not answer—could not. So she supplied
the answer herself.

'Today would be best, I think,' she said. 'Only—'
Her face suddenly constricted. 'Amelie… Amelie will
be upset. She's become…become very fond of me…'
She shut her eyes. 'And I of her,' she whispered.

She seemed to tremble, and it took all the strength he possessed to stay where he was.

'I'll make sure she understands,' he said. His voice sounded curt, even to himself.

He turned away. He could take no more of this. Not one fraction of a second more. He pulled open the schoolroom door again and was gone.

And in his head he heard Berenice's vicious, mocking laughter.

Behind him, unseen by him, Jenna slowly, very slowly, finished putting the exercise books into the cupboard, closed the door. Then slowly, very slowly, she sank to the ground, her arms clenched around her knees, tears flowing from her eyes, agony slicing across her heart.

How can he do this to me? So brutally—so callously? Have I been nothing to him, nothing at all?

Her eyes lifted in stark anguish. She remembered how ruthlessly he'd despatched Bianca from his life.

He was kinder to her than he was to me—wishing her well...

She gave a choke, her face buckling, tears scalding. Pain searing like red-hot pincers was breaking her heart in two with the agony of Evandro's indifferent coldness—and the agony of her trampled love.

Amelie broke into a storm of weeping. Evandro had collected her at the end of summer camp and told her Jenna was leaving.

'But I don't want her to go! I don't want her to!'

she sobbed wildly. 'I want her to stay here with us, Papà!'

Her tear-stained face pleaded with him, and little hands clutched at him desperately.

'Get her back, Papà! Please, please get her back!'

He pulled her to him, hugging her tightly. His heart wrung at her tearful grief.

'I can't, *mignonne*. I can't.'

She can never come back.

CHAPTER TWELVE

JENNA LET HERSELF into her flat. It was airless and stuffy, so she went around opening the windows as mechanically as she'd sorted Amelie's books that morning. As mechanically as she'd closed the schoolroom cupboard door after Evandro had left the room and her useless, pointless tears had dried. And as mechanically as she'd gone up to her bedroom and packed her clothes.

Not the ones Evandro had bought her. They were not hers. They were for a woman she no longer was.

The woman who longed for the heart's desire she could never have. Who longed for a family she could never have. Who longed for love from a man who would never love her.

Agony had sliced across her heart again— an agony she'd been able to do nothing about. Because there had been nothing more for her to do except what she'd been doing. Nothing more for her to say except what she had said.

And one more thing. Something she could not leave undone.

Suitcase shut, passport and wallet in her hand-bag, she had gone through into Amelie's bedroom. Pain had twisted inside her—and pity for the child she was leaving, who would come home to find her gone.

An ancient memory had haunted the edges of her mind—being told that her mother had been killed in a road accident. Told that she would be going to live with her father now, an unknown stranger to her.

But Amelie's father is not like mine. That is my comfort. She has a father who loves her dearly, as mine never did, who will always be there for her, always protect her, and for that she is blessed. And I was never her mother—only her teacher.

So it was as her teacher that she had left her note for Amelie, saying how well she'd done in all her schoolwork, how she hoped the little girl would enjoy her new school in the autumn.

I will always remember the lovely summer I spent here at this beautiful palazzo, *with you and your* papà. *Be good, poppet, and look after your* papà, *for he loves you very, very much...*

She hadn't been able to write any more, with her eyes blurring, tears scalding again. Tears for the little girl she had come to love whom now she would never see again.

Nor would she see the man she loved either.

Because she was invisible to him once again.

* * *

Evandro's eyes went to Amelie, where she was playing with the dolls' house he'd bought her in Naples. She was pushing furniture around, rearranging rooms, but her manner was listless,

'She's unhappy,' his aunt said, following his line of gaze into her drawing room. They were sitting out on the balcony of her spacious apartment overlooking the Bay of Naples. Her eyes came back to her nephew, waiting for an answer. An explanation.

None came.

'You told me she'd adjusted very well to life here with you in Italy,' his aunt persisted. 'So, why is she unhappy?'

Evandro knew he must say something—but he also knew his aunt never minced her words. She certainly hadn't about his marriage, taking an instant dislike to his bride when she'd met her for the first time on Evandro's wedding day, and surveying with foreboding her young nephew's dazzled expression as he'd poured champagne for Berenice, who'd tilted her head at him coquettishly, eyes glittering with seductive promise, keeping him in hapless thrall...

'I repeat—why is the child unhappy?'

His aunt's sharp voice was insistent, breaking in on his grim reverie.

Evandro sought to make his voice offhand. 'She's missing her teacher—the one I hired for the summer to bring Amelie up to scratch for starting school this autumn. That's why I thought it a good idea to bring her here—to get to know you. I thought a change of scene might help.'

His words rang hollow, and his aunt looked at him shrewdly.

'There was an article,' she said, with a speculative edge in her voice, her eyes never leaving him, 'in one of those wretched tabloids you used to feature in so regularly once that witch of a wife was out of your hair, when you were always celebrating your freedom with some sultry piece or other! Except…' her voice changed '…this last article was different. And so was the female it mentioned.'

She looked at him, sipping her martini, waiting for his answer.

Again, it didn't come.

She eyed him straight on. 'It isn't just Amelie who misses her teacher, is it?'

He looked away, unable to meet his aunt's too-perceptive eyes, but not before he saw her expression change.

'You fool, Evandro! Oh, you fool!' she said softly.

But he did not need telling. He was fortune's fool—and had been since the moment he had married Berenice.

He was never to be free of her malignity.
Never.

Jenna was job-hunting, scrolling through the vacant teaching positions advertised online. She would move away—out of London. North, south, east, west… It didn't matter where.

Because there was only one place where she longed to be. A place that was barred to her for ever now. Barred to her by the one man she wanted to be with. And never could be again. The one place she'd wanted with all her heart, all her being, to be her home…a place to belong to…to be part of… And the one man she'd wanted with all her heart, all her being, to be hers. And she his.

She saw them, vivid in her mind, as real as if she were there. Saw the gracious *palazzo*, the sun-lit terrace, the beautiful gardens, the shady woods above, the verdant valley below. Saw Loretta and Maria, bustling about, Signora Farrafacci sailing in her stately fashion through the beautiful rooms… and little Amelie running down the stairs, skipping along the terrace, riding her pink bicycle, handle-bar ribbons flying, calling out in her piping voice, rushing up to hug her…

And always Evandro—striding out to the terrace, lounging back in his dining chair at the head of the table, sweeping me into his arms, lowering his mouth to mine…

She saw it all—but it was as if she were a ghost, drifting through the scene, seeing it but invisible to those in front of her. An outsider with no right to be there, no right to belong.

No right to love them all…

She gave a cry of anguish, pressing her hand to her mouth as if she could silence it. Silence all that clamoured within her—stifle and smother the searing agony of longing for what could never be again.

* * *

Evandro glanced at his watch. Amelie was staying on late at school today—something to do with
choir practice, he recalled. He would fetch her later.
Maybe take her out to supper. Something to cheer
her up. Though she was settling down at the convent school, he still too often saw a doleful expression on her face.

But at least she was mentioning Jenna less. He
was grateful for that—and not just for Amelie's sake.

No, he would not go there. Refused to go back
there. To that very last moment when he'd stood in
the schoolroom and told Jenna what he had. Brief
and to the point.

It had been the best way to end it.

And she had gone. Packed her bag and left the
palazzo as if she had never been there. Slipping away
quietly, self-effacingly. Just…disappearing.

Invisible once more.

Now it was just he and Amelie making their home
here in the *palazzo*.

He was doing his best to encourage Amelie to
make new friends, exchange play dates, get involved
with all the activities the school offered—like the
choir practice she was at today.

As for himself, he was working from the *palazzo*
as much as possible, although he still needed to be
in Turin sometimes as well—still needed to allow
for some essential business travel. But Amelie was
fine here with his housekeeper and the staff to look
after her when he was away, and he always spent

time talking with her on the phone every evening, always brought her back a little present when he came home to the *palazzo*.

He was arranging his life around her, doing everything he could for her to ensure her happiness. Whatever had to be done.

Everything that I have to. Everything. Whatever the cost.

His mouth twisted, indenting the lines around it more deeply.

A doting father indeed...

With a jerking movement, he reached for the phone. He had business calls to make, and the afternoon was nearly over. What use was it to think of what it had cost him—of the price he had paid?

No use. It had cost, and he had paid. That was all there was to it.

Face shuttered, he started to key in the number he needed. But before he could connect there was a knock on the library door. Not the usual brief tap that presaged the entry of Signora Farrafacci with his coffee, but a sharper, heavier rap against the wood. And when she came in he could see at once that her usual calm demeanour was agitated.

'What is it?' he asked, frowning. He knew his housekeeper had been taken aback by Jenna's abrupt departure, but he had not encouraged any discussion of the matter and she knew better than to ask.

She came up to his desk now, definitely agitated. 'There's...there's someone arrived,' she said. Her voice was discernibly breathless, her bosom heaving. 'Demanding to see you.'

Evandro's frown deepened. 'Who?' he said. His first thought was Amelie—that something had happened to her. Alarm stabbed at him. And then a very, very different emotion.

Signora Farrafacci's bosom heaved again. 'It's...' She hesitated, then spat it out. 'Signora Rocceforte!'

Evandro froze.

Jenna stared out over the water. Its grey mass was smooth, giving no hint of the hidden turbulence beneath as the incoming tide met the outflowing current at this confluence of river and sea. On the far side of the wide estuary the low Kentish shore was almost indistinguishable from the level water.

She thrust her hands into the pockets of her jacket. Autumn was shortening the days, and the cool air already hinted at winter's incoming cold. This estuarine stretch of the Thames—in the Essex commuter town where she had found a temporary teaching position to cover an unexpected maternity leave—was not a landscape she knew, and its marshy reaches were bleak for all but the myriad seabirds that found refuge there.

Was it a similar refuge to the one she sought? Refuge from pain...from memory. From what might have been but never was. Never could be.

She made herself keep walking along the embankment, deserted except for dog walkers in the gathering dusk. An east wind, low but chill, keened over the water and she welcomed its scouring, as if it could scour out memory as well. And pain. And loss. And abject misery.

She quickened her pace. She must not wallow in her misery, must not endlessly bewail her loss.

I have to make a new life—I have to. Have to accept that I filled my head with illusions, creating a false reality for myself—false hopes and false longings. I wanted to belong to Evandro—to be the woman he loved—but I never did and eventually he rejected and ejected me.

Deliberately she made herself replay the moment of her dismissal. The brief brutality of it. Evandro just standing there, telling her it was an 'opportune' moment for her to go. Eliminating her from his life. His bed. Packing her off with nothing more than a few brief words.

She felt her hands clench in her pockets, half with pain and half with anger.

I did not deserve such treatment! Such indifferent brusqueness. Such a callous termination of what there had been between us. Especially coming out of nowhere...

She halted, frowning.

But had it?

The blow he'd inflicted in those brief, unbearable moments had been so overwhelming she had not been able to see out from under it. Now she forced herself to replay the nightmare scene.

He had told her he had heard from his aunt, inviting him and Amelie to visit her. Was that what that letter had been about? The one that had been in the mail that morning? The one that he had picked up before he got to his feet, tersely excusing himself, striding indoors?

She remembered how she'd stared after him... how she'd felt cold pooling inside her. Remembered the worry spreading through her.

Something is wrong, she'd thought.

She heard the words again now, echoing in her memory.

What could have been so wrong about a letter of invitation from an aunt?

She frowned again. But *had* that letter been from his aunt? It hadn't looked like the kind of letter an aunt would send... She screwed her eyes shut, trying to see it again in her mind. A large white envelope, businesslike, with the address printed, not handwritten, which surely an elderly aunt would have done, if she was writing to a family member? And the stamp...

Her eyes widened suddenly, as she dredged up subconscious memory.

Not Italian—French.

French?

But he'd said his aunt lived in Sorrento.

On sudden impulse she wheeled about, reversing her direction. It was as though a tide had turned within her, pushing back against the current sweeping her out into a drowning sea of loss and heartbreak. A new tide that brought new thoughts.

Protest rose in her like a litany.

The Evandro who sent me packing like that, so callously and uncaringly, is not the Evandro that I know. Not the Evandro with sardonic deadpan humour...the Evandro who openly enjoyed my company, my conversation. Not the Evandro who took me into his arms, his bed...his life! Who kissed me, and embraced me, and laughed with me, and held me close...so close...

The Evandro she knew was nothing like the blank-faced man who had looked across the schoolroom at her, terse and brusque, callous and uncaring, the lines around his mouth scored deeply, his eyes dark and shuttered. Sending her away as if there had been nothing between them—nothing at all. Sending her away as if compelled to do so...

By what?

And into her head came the words that had fallen from her lips that very first evening she had dined with him and Amelie.

'Under a malign spell.'

Her mind worked through it all. His marriage had been a disaster. She knew that—all the household knew that! But he was free of it and Amelie, his precious daughter, was with him now, safe and protected from her damaging, self-obsessed mother. There was nothing more that Berenice could do to harm him.

Or was there?

Jenna kept walking and picked up her pace, a sense of urgency filling her.

* * *

Evandro sat in the library, in the leather armchair set beside the unlit fireplace. The late October night was still mild, but it was unlit for another reason as well.

He had no wish to see flames of any kind, nor to catch the choking smell of smoke.

His grip on his brandy glass tightened and he took another mouthful. On the marble mantelpiece the steady ticking of the clock marked the seconds, the time that was passing so slowly. It was long past the midnight hour and silence had engulfed the house.

He finished his brandy, reached for the decanter, refilled his glass. He should stop drinking, but he was of no mind to do so.

He shut his eyes, resting his head back on the chair, face set. His jaw ached and he moved to touch his left cheek with his hand, then let it drop, not willing to feel the pain that still throbbed beneath the analgesic of alcohol. He took another mouthful of brandy instead, stretching out his legs stiffly, trying not to wince at the effort it took.

If he drank enough he might fall asleep here, in the chair. It would be better than going to bed. Better than lying there in its wide expanse. Alone except for memories. A savage self-mockery slashed across his mind. Those never left him alone.

Too many memories. Too bitter to bear. Too unbearable.

Memories of a woman he would never see again. Who was beyond him for ever.

For ever.

The damning words scythed across him, cutting deep into his core. His very being. All that was left of it…

Emotion seared him like flame across flesh already burnt and scorched. It was agonising.

In sudden, furious, unbearable desolation, he hurled his brandy glass into the fireplace. It shattered, but he did not hear the noise. Heard only a tearing, abject cry go up that was like the roar of a wounded beast, piercing the floor of heaven.

He only dimly realised that the noise had come from him.

Jenna jackknifed upright, eyes flaring open wide, heart pounding, instantly awake.

A dream—that was all it had been. A dream. But that cry, torn from a human soul…

A dream—only a dream!

But a dream so real, so vivid, that it was still there—and she was still in it. She tried to shake her head, to make herself wake out of it, but she could not. Her eyes were open, but it was not the bedroom she was seeing.

She heard her ragged breathing, felt her hands digging into the mattress, the headboard pressing into her spine. Her hectic heart rate did not ease, and it was still pounding as she got out of bed and went to the window, dragging back the curtains of her bedsit to stare out over the street, deserted now, with midnight long past, as though she might see out there what was in her head.

Then, numbly, she turned away.

A dream, she told herself again. That terrible broken cry was only a dream.

But what if it wasn't?

It was absurd to think so—irrational. And yet the dream she'd woken from had been so all-consuming that she needed to do something…anything…that might calm her.

Shakily, she reached for her laptop, hunkering down in her bed again and logging in, ignoring the late hour. She had to be at school tomorrow to teach, but sleep was beyond her now.

What she was searching for she did not know, but as if of their own accord she found her fingers typing the words 'Evandro Rocceforte' into the search engine. Halfway down the first page of results an article title leapt out at her.

Dread filled her as she clicked on the link and started to read. It was a press release from Rocceforte Industriale.

It is with regret that we announce the resignation of chairman and chief executive Evandro Rocceforte, owing to ill health. In his place he has appointed…

She read no more as icy, terrifying fear filled her.

CHAPTER THIRTEEN

JENNA STOOD BY the side of the road where the local bus had deposited her. She had not been able to find a taxi in the town, and now the steep driveway up to the *palazzo* awaited her.

At least she had no luggage. That would have been an imposition—a presumption too far. A major part of her still told her that she was being insane to do what she had done—phoning the school to tell them that she would not be in today, then heading for Southend airport, taking the first flight out to Bergamo and then catching the train onwards.

But fear had driven her—and the searing memory of that terrible dream. And then the announcement she had read.

What 'ill health'?

She felt fear clutch at her again, overriding everything else. Overriding the impulsive insanity of what she was doing and driving her onwards with a terrifying question.

What ill health would make him resign from the

*business that he was head of? He would never have
done so lightly...*

She headed up the narrow drive, quickening her
pace, her thoughts still as jumbled as they had been
since last night.

*That letter he received...his swift and brutal
dismissal of me...my feeling that something was
wrong...and now this announcement of 'ill health'.
Was it bad news about his health that was in that
letter? Was that why he got rid of me?*

The questions tumbled through her brain, clash-
ing with her fear and heightening it.

As she neared the sharp bend where the rocky outcrop forced the roadway around it, memory washed
over her of that very first night—of running into
the path of Evandro's speeding car to save him from
danger.

It had been an impulse—instant and overriding.
Just as this insanely executed journey was now.

She rounded the outcrop, striding onwards, ignoring the place where the drive continued on to the
front of the *palazzo* and instead taking the shorter
path cutting through the woods to the gardens behind. Just before she left the woods—before she
allowed herself to look at the *palazzo*—she felt her
eyes go to where the lightning-struck chestnut stood,
cloven in two.

The branches that had trailed on the ground had
been cleared, the burnt limbs severed, but the trunk
of the tree remained, blackened and scorched. Dead
and stricken and lifeless. And yet around the base...

Her eyes rested there now, and emotion flooded her at the sight. New shoots were growing…

She let her gaze slip past it, down over the beautiful gardens to the *palazzo*'s façade.

It was as elegant, as perfectly proportioned as it always had been, with its symmetrical pediments and rows of sash windows catching the sunlight, the French doors opening up to the spacious terrace all along its length.

Exactly as she remembered it.

Exactly as she had dreamt it last night.

Exactly as it had always been.

Except—

Shock and horror jarred through her. The rear elevation of the *palazzo* was exactly as it always had been. And so was one room deep behind the enfilade of French doors. But beyond that—

Beyond that the entire frontage of the *palazzo* was a blackened shell, the marble-floored entrance hall half open to the sky. And in the air, acrid and dry, was the faint smell of smoke and ash and ruin.

Numb, disbelieving, she walked down through the gardens, feeling her heart pounding harder and faster with every step. As she gained the terrace a figure stepped out from the *palazzo*'s interior.

She gave a cry, her hand flying to her mouth.

Evandro stilled, turning his head.

That cry…

She was coming towards him, walking with a rapidity that was bringing her closer with every burning second. She blurred, going in and out of focus.

The last woman in the world he wanted to see him.

The only woman in the world he wanted to see.

And then she was there—in front of him. A woman who should not be there, who had no reason to be there…no cause. A woman who was looking at him with horror on her face.

'Dear God…' she said, breathing shallowly.

Her eyes, those clear pools as cool and as green as the shade under the canopy of trees where they'd held each other, were wide and fearful.

He felt his face twist. 'God,' he said, and his voice was harsh, 'had very little to do with it.'

He looked at her. His focus was poor, but forcibly he made it work—such as it could now. A snap of pain flashed across his face—it felt like agony.

'Why have you come?'

That harshness was still in his voice, and he saw her flinch. But perhaps not on account of his voice alone.

She simply looked at him. 'I had to,' she said.

He saw her expression change as she tried to make sense of the sight in front of her.

'I heard you call out,' she said. 'In a dream.' Her words were disjointed. She stopped…went on again. 'Then I looked you up online. I found an article that said you had resigned from your company. Ill health, it said. But it didn't…it didn't say…'

She halted, and in her eyes were the things he would see in all eyes now. Must always see.

Pity—and horror.

'How…?' She swallowed, stopped.

He took a breath. 'Come inside, if you will,' he said. His voice was less harsh, now merely grating. 'I need to sit down,' he went on. 'Walking is still… difficult. As you can see.'

He indicated the cane in his right hand which could not stop him limping heavily, as he did now, heading indoors with a halting, painful gait. He went back into the library, sinking down with relief, loosening his hunched shoulders as he sank into the deep leather chair by the unlit hearth, indicating that she should take the chair opposite.

She did so, sitting down abruptly. He could still see the shock on her face—the pity and the horror.

'Tell me,' she said.

There was a plea in her voice. He did not need her to spell out what she wanted him to tell her.

He set his cane aside, leaning it carefully against the mantel and stretching out his legs. The bones that had been crushed by falling masonry, which were knitting together again slowly and painfully, made the movement difficult.

His voice was bleak as he answered her, hard and terse. 'My wife came calling,' he said.

He saw Jenna stare.

His mouth twisted. 'My ex-wife,' he corrected. 'Though she never accepted that. She insisted on staying the night.' His voice was expressionless now. 'Ideally with me.'

He heard Jenna gasp, but carried on, letting his eyes rest on her, forcing them to focus by effort of will.

'When I…declined…her invitation, she retired, furious, to her room—one of the guest bedrooms at the front had been made up for her—and proceeded to demand dinner and bottles of vintage champagne, wine and liqueurs, all of which she demolished.' His voice became devoid of emotion. 'So that when she neglected to properly extinguish one of her cigarettes and it dropped to the floor, it smouldered on the rug before working its way along her discarded clothes to reach the curtains.'

He paused before going on.

'The smoke alarms went off, waking the household, summoning the fire service. But the town is some way off, as you know. And fire,' he said, 'spreads very swiftly in old houses.'

He fell silent, his blurring gaze dropping to the fireplace, filling it, in his mind's eye, with the inferno that burned in his head all the time now. The memory of the roar of flames and the crack of burning timbers, the choking, suffocating smoke…

He lifted his gaze again, resting it on Jenna. She looked bleak, unreadable.

'I tried to save her. Allow me that, if you will. I had wished her to hell—but not…' his voice twisted again '…not like that.'

He worked to find the right words.

'They say she died of smoke inhalation, and that because she had already passed out with so much alcohol in her system she would have known little of what was happening to her.' He paused again. 'She's been interred. The family plot in the churchyard. For decency's sake. For Amelie's sake—' he broke off.

'*Amelie*. Please tell me she didn't witness…' Fearful concern filled her voice.

'She was away,' he told her. 'The moment Berenice showed up I phoned the school to ask them to keep her with the boarders that night. Then, afterwards, it was impossible for her to come back until the place was made safe and I was out of hospital. But she's back here now, going to school every day—they thought it best for her to keep as much as possible to her normal routine. To minimise trauma.'

Jenna's clear-water eyes lifted to his. 'And you?' she asked quietly. 'Your trauma?'

'I'm alive,' he said. 'That is all that matters.' He stilled. 'For Amelie.'

Something flickered in her face. Something his damaged eyesight could not make out.

'Not just for Amelie,' she said.

And then, before his vision blurred again, he saw tears start to seep from the forest pools that were her eyes and flow silently down her cheeks.

She could not stop. The silent flow was impossible to halt. And why should she try and halt it? Why shouldn't she weep?

He tried to save her—tried to save the woman

who had tormented him for so many years, who so recklessly endangered not just herself but everyone here. In spite of it all, he still tried to save her— risking his life for hers. At such a cost.

Through the tears she could not stop she beheld his scarred and ravaged face. The left-hand side showed emergency skin grafts, and the jagged slash across his left eye was like a livid lightning bolt. The cane propped beside him acted both as guide for his damaged vision and support for his shattered leg.

Pity constricted in her—and so much more than pity. Her heart overflowed with it.

He was holding out a handkerchief to her. It was large and made of a fine cotton, with his initials in the corner. There was a sardonic look in his eyes, a look so familiar she thought time had slipped and the past had enveloped her in its kindly embrace.

'Enough tears, Jenna,' he said. 'I'll survive. And you, of all people, should not weep for me.' His voice was harsh, but it was directed at himself, not her. 'Not after what I did to you.'

She saw the lines surrounding his mouth that she had once thought deep now scored like knife wounds, tightening to a whipped line.

'Not after that,' he said.

With a sudden movement Evandro got to his feet, unable to bear sitting there any longer. He crossed to his desk, not bothering to take his cane, his halting gait slowing him, frustrating him. He yanked open the drawer of his desk and took out the envelope that had sat there since the day he'd sent Jenna packing.

He felt a pain stab him that had nothing to do with the still-healing bones in his injured thigh, but he made himself ignore it—as he ignored all the physical punishment his once-strong body had taken that hellish night.

He stared for a moment at the envelope he was holding, propping himself against the front edge of the desk so that it supported him, taking the weight off his half-crippled leg. He looked across at her, saw her expression change.

'That letter...' he heard her say faintly. 'The one that came... I thought, when I read the announcement of your resignation, that the letter had been bad news...about the ill health the article mentioned...'

She spoke disjointedly, sitting very still, knees drawn together, hands clenched in her lap.

'Not ill health,' he corrected, his voice empty. 'Ill will—'

He broke off, but knew he must say more.

He drew a harsh and heavy breath. Forced himself on. 'There was a reason, Jenna, why I did what I did to you—why I sent you packing the way I did.' He paused, still reluctant to speak.

I never thought I would have to tell her. Never thought I would need to. Because I never thought I'd see her again—I thought that she was gone for ever from my life.

After all, hadn't that been his intention? The very purpose that had driven him, that dark day, up to

Amelie's schoolroom to do what he had? Sending her away, never to return?

Yet for reasons he could not fathom, dared not think about, she had returned to the *palazzo*. So he could not keep his silence while she sat there like that, with those useless, futile, wasted tears drying on her cheeks.

He took another breath, his tone changing. 'Jenna, understand this—ever since my divorce the tabloid press, the gossip columns, have made copy and headlines out of me. They get a helping hand—from Bianca, for one. She liked to tip them off when I was going about with her. Partly because she enjoyed being in the limelight and partly…' his eyes hardened '…because she hoped it might help in her goal of becoming the next Signora Rocceforte. She never had a chance, of course, but the hacks would have loved to break such a story. So when—'

He stopped. Then resumed resignedly. No point in starting this sorry tale only to bottle it now.

'There was a story, Jenna, published in one of the tabloid rags after we arrived back here from Turin— an article I never saw coming, which outlined how very different you are from the likes of Bianca, and explained your presence in my life in a very different way. The reporter attempted to paint you into the role Bianca never could attain—said that you were to me what she never had been nor ever could be. The consequence of which was…' he dropped the envelope on to his desk as if it were dangerous to touch '…this letter.'

He stared down at it now, heaviness crushing him. Then, like a switch, he snapped his eyes back to Jenna. She was sitting so still…so very, very still.

He made himself go on. Willing her to understand what he had done—why he had done it. Not so she would forgive him—never that—but so she would understand.

His damaged eyes rested on her. It hurt to see her. She was so close, yet so infinitely far away.

'Jenna, from the very first I knew it was…unwise… to be anything to you other than your employer and your pupil's father. Knew it was…unwise…to want anything more. Unwise to spend time with you, talk with you, laugh with you. Unwise to want you to shed your sad cloak of invisibility. Unwise to kiss you in the moonlight—'

His expression changed.

'That's why I put you from me—pushed you away. That's why I brought Bianca here with all her friends, wanting to banish my desire for you by flooding myself and my home with distraction. I thought it would help me to keep away from you. To undo what I had so unwisely begun.'

His eyes rested on her. She had not moved. Not one iota. She was as still as a statue made of living flesh.

He forced himself on. 'But I couldn't banish you from my thoughts, my longings. If anything, the whole endeavour only proved to me that it was *you* I wanted to be with, with every fibre of my being.'

His voice changed again. Dropped to a low intensity.

'You were everything that Berenice was not. You alone—of all the world—could draw from me the poison of my nightmare marriage. Your quiet ways and your quiet voice and your quiet loveliness… Your clear spring water eyes and your sylvan grace… And above all—oh, above all, Jenna, your honesty, your truthfulness, your kindness and your compassion. You were all that I craved—all I could not do without. You were the woman I wanted—needed—to make my life whole again.'

Into his head came the memory of standing out on the still-damp terrace after their first unforgettable night together, when he had made her his. Standing in the fresh morning sunshine after the storm that had devastated the chestnut tree, feeling the air that had been bright and clear and clean.

'The world new-made,' she had said.

He drew a breath, deep into his smoke-ravaged lungs. 'And so I cleared them all out—Bianca and her friends—and, heedless of the danger, came striding to claim you.' He shut his eyes. 'To make you mine.'

His eyes flashed open again.

'A dangerous word, Jenna…*mine*. And I knew the danger—God help me, I knew! Knew I should not claim you, knew I should be wise and never hold you in my arms, never kiss you, never sweep you into my bed, my life, my—'

He broke off. He shouldn't say any more. She had endured enough at his hands.

'I knew it,' he said instead, 'but I ignored it. Silenced it. Told myself I would take the risk even though I knew how real that risk would be, because of how very different from Bianca you were.'

He saw her expression change now. Saw a flickering that seemed to be a lightening and then a frown of puzzlement.

'Risk?' Her voice was strained and low. She was not understanding. 'What risk, Evandro? How?'

He tensed his jaw, sending pain shooting through the scars on his face. He was silent for a moment, his face grim. He did not want to tell her this—*por Dio*, he did not! But tell her he must.

'The risk,' he said, his voice like leaden stones, 'that I would have to choose.' He paused, looking at her, his eyes like weights upon her. 'Choose between you…and Amelie.'

Jenna heard the words but could not believe them.

'Evandro, I would never…never *dream* of…of—' She broke off, dismay at what he'd said vivid in her face. 'I would never, never make you do such a thing! How could you think it, Evandro? How could you think I would ever do anything to harm what you have with Amelie?'

She could hear the distress in her voice, along with the agitation and protest.

'How could you think, after everything I told you about how my own father chose my stepmother over me—rejecting me—that I would ever, *ever* want you to do that to Amelie? And why should I? Amelie is a darling! I love her as much as I love—' She broke off again, her face working. 'I would *never* make you choose.'

He held up a hand. 'Not you,' he said heavily. 'It would not be you making me choose—never you.'

Incomprehension furrowed her brow. 'But who?'

'Berenice,' he said flatly.

'Berenice?' Her incomprehension was total.

He pushed away from his desk, moved to sink down into the executive chair behind it,

'I have another sorry tale to tell you,' he opened, his voice still heavy. 'Ugly, but necessary.'

He seemed to hesitate, as if he had no wish to say what he must. Then, his expression steeling, he spoke, his voice harsh and grating.

'My father wanted to expand Rocceforte Industriale in a merger with a similar French company, Trans-Montane, which was in financial difficulties but which would have been a good match for us. Berenice had inherited a controlling interest in the company, so the obvious, easiest way for the merger to proceed was by...' he took a slicing breath '...by uniting our two families. To say I was in agreement would be an understatement.' There was scathing self-mockery in his voice now. 'I was happy to please my father—as I told you that day we had our tea party—and glad to do good for the company that had been in our family for over a hundred years, but I didn't marry for that reason alone.'

He paused again, and Jenna saw something in his face that stabbed at her. Heard a hollowing in his voice when he spoke next.

'I took one look at Berenice—and was lost.'

She saw him shift restlessly in his chair, heard the tension in his voice as he went on.

'I was twenty-five, full of romantic notions. My father was delighted. I would have a wife every man would envy me for, who would double our business overnight.' His voice changed, became etched with sadness now. 'And I would also bring him the joy of knowing that I was making a love match as wonderful as he had known—the match that had been taken from him by the death of my mother two years earlier. He wanted so much to see me happily married...to see me deeply in love—'

He broke off. Again Jenna saw something change in his face, becoming hard, twisting his mouth.

'As it happened, my wife wanted that too. She wanted me deeply in love with her. Besotted by her. She knew it would make me...malleable. Easy to manipulate. It was the same aim she had for all the hapless males she drew to her. But for me, her husband, it was even more important to keep me that love-struck, devoted fool who'd married her with stars in his eyes thinking he'd found his dream come true—his ravishing bride. She wanted me to be her faithful adoring husband, eagerly footing the bill for her every extravagance, lavishing everything she wanted upon her, doing anything for her—anything at all. Putting up with her capriciousness and her temper, her self-obsession and her narcissism, turning a blind and ever-forgiving eye to her constant affairs, indulging her in anything and everything she craved—and thinking myself privileged to be allowed to do so.'

His voice hardened even more.

'But although I'd thought the best of her when I'd married her, I came to see the worst of her. To see through her superficial allure, to see her for what she truly was—and she could not endure it. Was enraged by it. So she turned on all her powers to charm and seduce and beguile me, to draw me back into her manipulative clutches—determined not just to entrap me in her web again but to punish me for seeking to withdraw from her. Punish me,' he said grimly, 'by breaking my heart.'

He paused, his face emptying of all emotion.

'She could not do it,' he said. 'She could not make me stay love-struck for a woman who had no love for anyone, let alone her husband. She had lost her power over me. I stuck with her—tolerated her for Amelie's sake, even though I saw so little of her, and even for my father's sake. But after he died I knew I could endure it no longer. And when I divorced her it was the end of her power entirely. She was defeated. I was done with her.'

Jenna saw an expression form on his face that chilled her to the bone.

'But Berenice,' Evandro said, his words falling like stones, 'was not done with me.'

His eyes focused intently on hers as he went on, almost piercing her.

'And when I claimed custody of Amelie she struck.'

He looked away for a moment, as if seeing something far away that was out of reach to him. That always would be. Then his lasering gaze came back to her.

'My determination to wrest Amelie from her had shown her how much she could demand of me before she conceded custody—and it gave her a new power over me. Not just to force me to pay her a fortune for Amelie—over and above what I had already paid her for her divorce settlement—but to get something that would satisfy her even more. Would satisfy her lust for revenge on me for daring to reject her, escape her, divorce her. For denying her the pleasure of breaking my heart. *She* might not be able to break my heart herself—but she knew she could still break it using Amelie. It was the price,' he said, his voice empty of all emotion now, 'of finally conceding custody to me.'

She saw his darkened eyes flick to the letter he'd taken from the desk drawer and held up to her before discarding it on the desk's surface. Then his eyes came back to her.

'She demanded I sign a document that my lawyer was appalled by. He was horrified—and he warned me what she was intent on. "You are giving her the power to destroy your future," he told me. But I did not care. Could not. I knew it would give me Amelie and bring to an end the delays and prevarications and endless wrangling that Berenice was using to drag out the process. Amelie would come to me permanently. The custody battle would be over. Unless—'

Yet again, he broke off. Yet again, his gaze shifted away from her. And this time it did not come back to her as he continued to speak, as if his eyes were consciously avoiding her.

'She wanted to break my heart so she found a way. By making me choose…' and now his eyes lashed back to her '…choose between Amelie and any other woman who might come to mean something to me.' His face twisted. 'The likes of Bianca didn't bother her. She knew they were simply women for affairs—nothing more than that. But you—you, Jenna—were different. That damnable article in that tabloid, with its prurient speculation about who you were to me, reached her, and—just as I dreaded— she struck.'

His gaze dropped again to the letter lying on his desktop.

'It's from her lawyers,' he said. 'Relaunching the custody battle for Amelie—just as Berenice threatened she would. Unless—'

That word hung in the air again.

'Unless I did what I had agreed—what I'd promised in that document my lawyer was appalled by. And so I sent you packing.' He took a deep and weary breath. 'She forced me to choose. To choose between Amelie—and you.'

Emotion speared in Jenna as she heard his words, propelling her into speech just as it had before. 'That could never be a choice for you, Evandro! *Never.*'

Memory assailed her—not of that dreadful last day at the *palazzo*, but a memory much older than that. A memory of a father for whom that *had* been a choice. A father who had chosen very differently. Choosing his new wife and rejecting his daughter.

As Evandro never, never would.

As she would never want him to.

'No, it never could be.'

The words of this man, the father who had made a different choice from her own, echoed hers.

'It never could be. I could never hand Amelie back into Berenice's malign clutches—never betray the vow I made to protect her from her toxic mother always, no matter the cost. So I did what her lawyer's letter demanded,' he said, his voice emptying. 'I pushed you away. Despatched you back to England. Finished with you. End of—'

The staccato words fell away from him.

There was too much in Jenna's head—far too much. Swirling like a maelstrom, her emotions were chaotic, and she felt entirely overwhelmed. But out of it all, one thing crystallised. One thing that made no sense. No sense at all after everything he'd told her. Something that furrowed her brow, made her get to her feet and go halfway towards his desk, then halt.

Her gaze dropped momentarily to the thick white envelope on the desk in front of him, with its typed address, its French stamp, its letter inside containing its cruel demand—Berenice's final vengeance on the man she had already wronged so much…her final threat to the child she had used as a weapon against her loving father. Then her eyes lifted to Evandro—to his ravaged face and the bleakness in his damaged eyes. She felt emotion move within her, but suppressed it. This was not the moment for it.

She felt her frown deepen, her troubled thoughts turn questioning. She took a breath, trying to make sense of something that made *no* sense. No sense at all. And when she spoke, her voice was filled with incomprehension.

'Everything you've told me about Berenice,' she began, picking her words carefully, 'everything Signora Farrafacci has let slip about her, everything that Amelie herself has said—and, even now, the way you described the horror of her death and how she brought it about by her irresponsible recklessness… Everything from Amelie's chaotic, unstable life with her—so absolutely unsuitable for a child—to her using Amelie as a bargaining chip in your divorce to extract a fortune from you, to her hedonism, extravagance, narcissism, selfishness and self-regard—her perpetual infidelities and her drinking… Everything points, surely, to her having had no chance at all at reversing the custody decision. So, how…' she took a laboured breath '…*how* could she ever have threatened you and Amelie in that way?'

Her voice was vehement.

'Evandro, what judge in the world—in any jurisdiction!—would hand Amelie back to such a mother? Would take her away from her father—'

He cut across her. His voice stark. 'But I'm not Amelie's father.'

CHAPTER FOURTEEN

JENNA STILLED, eyes fixed on Evandro.

'I am not Amelie's father,' he said again.

Something seemed to pass across his face, then it was gone.

'Just who is will probably never be known. Not even to Berenice.' His voice held no emotion. 'As for DNA tests—well, the choice of candidates would be very broad. And international. Berenice had no interest in identifying him. She only threw the unedifying information my way when she saw me with the baby that up until then she had let me think was mine.' His expression was as harsh as his voice. 'The baby I'd hoped, so much, might mark a turning point for us. At that point my refusal to give up completely on the shambles of my marriage was being fed by my delusions that a child between us might salvage something decent and true. But when Berenice saw me cradling Amelie—a typical doting Italian father—it so enraged her to have me paying attention to anyone but herself that she threw at me, with sadistic mockery, the news that I was devoting myself to another man's bastard.'

His expression changed again.

'I knew that our marriage was over then. But the real cruelty of that moment was not in what she had thrown at me, but in the fact that there was now, in that unholy, toxic mess, a child… A child innocent of all the sordid circumstances of her conception and her birth, now trapped in the poisonous web of Berenice's jealousy, spite and self-obsession.'

Jenna saw him take another breath, ragged and harsh.

'The truth of Amelie's parentage became her ultimate weapon against me.'

He looked away, out over the terrace, as if he were watching Amelie playing out there, riding her pink bicycle up and down, golden hair streaming. The golden hair which she now knew came neither from Berenice nor Evandro. Jenna had finally got an answer to that question, it seemed.

'It was a weapon that would win her everything she wanted—the fact that I had no legal right to a child I loved, because she was not mine. Her rage at being usurped by another female in my life, her fury that I'd dared to see her for what she was, all found a weapon in Amelie's paternity. It was a gun perpetually pointed at me. And not just pointed at me— pointed at a victim far more vulnerable. At Amelie.'

He paused, his voice as tight as a garrotte.

'All she had to do was tell the court I was not Amelie's father and demand a DNA test to prove it.

My claim for sole custody would crumble.' His voice tightened even more. 'Even if a judge had ruled her an unfit mother, Amelie would have been taken into care, lost in a system that, yes, might…*might*…have allowed me to adopt her—eventually—but after how much wrangling? How lengthy a process? But there was no certainty of that—none. Remember, I had never had more than minimal contact with Amelie—Berenice had seen to that, keeping perpetually on the move as she dragged the child around Europe and America, preventing me from forming a relationship with her. And even with Amelie in care, Berenice might have tried to regain custody of her. As I have bitter cause to know, she could be supremely manipulative and convincing—she would have done whatever it had taken to get Amelie back for the sole purpose of tormenting me, taunting me, knowing how desperately I wanted to save Amelie from her. How desperately responsible I felt for her.'

His voice emptied.

'I was Berenice's target—it was me she wanted to make suffer. But it would have been Amelie who'd be her victim. And I was responsible for that. If I hadn't shown Berenice how much I'd come to despise her, if I hadn't sought my freedom from the hell of our marriage, I might have been able to protect Amelie, or at least mitigate Berenice's damaging influence. But when she knew I was determined to break free from her, she wanted to use Amelie against me. And I could not allow that—could not abandon her to Berenice. I had to fight for her.'

Something moved in his eyes—a flash of emotion that pierced Jenna to the core. Emotion was rising in her like a tide she could not stop.

'I've tried...' he said, his voice low.

He was not looking at Jenna, but into himself, and Jenna could see his hands, as viciously scarred as his face, clench over the arms of his chair.

'I've tried to be the best father I could to Amelie—even though I'm not her father. To do the best I can for her. Because she deserves whatever even a non-father like me can do for her. Because she has no one else to protect her but me! I know I'm *not* her father, but—'

The emotion she could not stop—would not now have stopped for all the world itself—broke in Jenna. She surged forward, carried on that unstoppable emotion, her hands slamming down on the desk.

Her eyes were blazing, her voice vehement. 'You *are* her father! You are her father in *every* way that counts. Do you think it takes DNA to make a father? My father gave me his DNA and nothing else. He never stood by me. He abandoned my mother, smashed our family to pieces by running off with another woman, and then treated me, when I was forced upon him, with coldness and resentment and rejection. He didn't care. He *never* cared about me. But *you* care. You care about Amelie and you love her—love her in every moment you spend with her, every hug you give her, every smile, each and every one. It is *love*, Evandro, *love* that makes you her father. *Love*.'

She had to make him believe it, accept what she was saying as true. Her voice was fierce with urging—with urgency.

'Love,' she said again, more quietly, but no less insistently, her eyes holding his, blazing still. 'Love and loyalty. The undying, unbreakable loyalty of a father—a true father, as you are, Evandro, and as you always will be—who places his child's happiness above and beyond everything else. You've stood by her through everything Berenice did or tried to do. You *are* Amelie's father, Evandro, in every vital meaning of the word—and no power in heaven or earth can say otherwise. None.'

She knew the blaze was still in her eyes, because she had to make him accept what she had said—it was the most important thing in the world to her. But it was a blaze that was becoming a glow—a glow to fill her heart. And not just hers.

She saw his eyes close, lashes splayed on his cheeks, and she could see the tension racking his shoulders begin to ease, see the veins standing out on the backs of his scarred hands relieved as his clenched grip loosened. He bowed his head for a moment, then lifted it again, opening his eyes.

Joltingly, he levered himself to his feet, coming around the desk to her. She turned towards him, but he remained a few feet away.

'Thank you,' he said, his voice low. 'And thank you for…for understanding.' The strain in his voice was audible. 'For knowing why…why I had to choose Amelie—'

He broke off, and looked away, as if he could not bear to look at her. She felt emotion turn and twist within her.

'I wish you had told me, Evandro. Told me what Berenice was threatening. I would have understood—I would have left at once. You would not have needed to tell me to go.'

Let alone in the brutal, callous way you did.

A silent cry sounded within her. She'd told herself, convinced herself while walking by the Thames, that the man who had severed her from his life so dismissively could not be the same man she had found such happiness with. That something was wrong. It had been a feeling so strong and overpowering that it had triggered that terrifying dream last night, compelling her to come here to discover this scene of devastation and destruction.

But to what purpose?

The question mocked her, pain stabbing again.

For herself—none, she realised with bitter pain.

In my dream he was calling for me. But it was only in my dream—in my own longing. I was foolish to hope it could ever be real.

Because for all that he had told her now, and for all the longing in her—seeing the terrible scars on his face, the pain from his mangled leg etched in his face—to take him into her arms, to shelter him from what he had endured with all the love she felt for him, he obviously didn't feel the same way.

He has not swept me into his arms—taken me back.

She forced the realisation into her head, cruel though it was.

He'd moved on from women like Bianca, who'd been necessary for him to regain his freedom after Berenice.

Moved on to me—because I helped him build the relationship with Amelie he needed to make. Because I brought him comfort after all he'd been through—helped him put his tormented past behind him so that he could move on again—move on from me. He will never love me as I love him. Never want me as I want him.

It hurt so much to think it, to know it, but she had to face it. Face it and accept it. Anguish filled her, an anguish that she knew she'd carry with her all her life... And then, dimly, she realised he had started to speak.

'But I *did* need to tell you to go, Jenna,' he said.

His voice was still harsh, and she wondered at it.

'I needed to tell you—and in the callous way that I did.'

She looked at him, not understanding.

'Because,' he told her, 'I needed to make you hate me.'

She stepped back. Expression blank. His words did not make sense.

'Jenna, I didn't tell you about Berenice's threat because I knew what you would say—that you would never dream of urging me to do anything but concede to it. You would leave me for Amelie's sake, never thinking to do otherwise. And there was nothing I could do. Except what I did.'

He took a scissoring breath, as if forcing himself to go on.

'It was the only way to make sure you left me feeling relief. Relief at being shot of a man who could end his relationship with you in such a brutal manner.'

He looked away for a moment, as if reluctant to look at her, to see her standing there, hearing what he was telling her. Then his gaze snapped back to her.

'It was the best thing I could do for you, Jenna— make you hate me so that you would be free to find someone worthy of you.' He stopped, took another scissoring breath. 'And you will, Jenna. You *will* find someone worthy of you.'

His words pierced her, like arrows burying themselves in her twice-broken heart. The heart that had broken when he'd sent her away. The heart that had broken again, just now, when she'd realised that even though Berenice and the threat she posed were gone, he was still sending her away, willing her to meet another man—a man who was not him.

Cold, empty, bleak despair filled her. She should go—and now. That would be best. She had no place here—not any more. She was unwanted and unloved. Unnecessary to him. He'd made that clear. Was making it clearer still as she heard what he was saying now, his words less halting, more resolute, and her heart tore in two all over again, the grief of it overwhelming her.

'It was good that you returned to England when you did, Jenna. Back to your own life.'

He placed a hand down on the surface of the desk, as if he needed the support, and went on speaking, though his voice seemed to be coming from very far away. From a distant place that was beyond her reach and always would be.

'A life that is yours and yours alone. A life that, one day, you will share with someone you can give your heart to.'

He turned away abruptly, limping with painful strides towards the doors to the terrace, one arm outstretched towards the door jamb to help take the weight off his damaged leg. He looked back towards her, his face strained, sunlight from the terrace throwing into stark relief the livid scarring from his burns, the puckered skin around his half-blind eye.

And there was something in the expression in his face now, as his eyes went to her, that was like a sudden vice around her broken heart. What was in his face was unbearable to see—and it was not because of his terrible scars.

'Berenice came here that day to gloat,' he said. 'To celebrate her victory over me—the fact that I had yielded to her threat. But if her death took that power from her it gave her another. Her final triumph.'

The bitterness in his voice lacerated Jenna.

'It made me the maimed and crippled wreck that I am now.'

* * *

Evandro turned away again, staring half blindly out
over the unspoilt gardens of the *palazzo*, bathed in
autumnal sunlight. At the garden's edge he could
see the chestnut that had been struck by lightning
the night he had presumed to make Jenna his own.
The burnt and sagging limbs had been cut back, but
the tree's blackened, divided trunk was still standing. Scorched and stricken.

As I am.

Bitterness assailed him again.

Even from the grave Berenice's malignity still
reached him.

He released the door jamb, painfully turned to
face into the room again. To face the woman he did
not want to face. Whom he wished with all his being
had never come here. Had never seen him like this.

He steeled his jaw. But it was good that she was
seeing him like this—so she would know how
Berenice had parted them from each other.

He let his eyes rest on her.

One last time.

In the silence he could hear the ticking of the
clock on the mantel over the fire. He frowned. Amelie would be home from school soon—and she must
not see Jenna. It was imperative that she did not.

'Jenna.' He spoke abruptly, limping towards her.
He needed his damn cane, his leg was aching as he
walked without it. 'You need to leave. Amelie will
be back soon and I don't want her—' He stopped. 'I
don't want her seeing you. It would…upset her.' He

took a razoring breath. 'She would think you had come back. To stay.'

He saw her swallow, then nod. There seemed to be something wrong with her face. It must be the strain of looking at him, trying not to let her pity and revulsion show. He wanted to laugh—mocking the gods as they now mocked him. Or was it just Berenice mocking him?

His lawyer's warning sounded in his ears, as it had so many times.

'You're giving her the power to destroy your future.'

His mouth twisted.

And she has—she has destroyed my future. Destroyed it from the grave.

Jenna was speaking, her voice low, and as strained as the expression on her face. How slight she looked, how pale. Her face was as white as it had been the night she'd sat in the corner of the salon while Bianca and her friends had partied all around her.

Looking as though her world had ended.

'I'm sorry, Evandro,' she was saying now. 'So very, very sorry. Sorry for all…all this…' She stumbled on her words. 'I even wish I could feel sorry for Berenice,' he heard her say. 'But I can't. However dreadful her end—' She broke off, pressed her hand to her forehead. 'God must forgive her,' she whispered, 'for I can't. Not for what she caused to happen to you—not just through all the years of your marriage, but now—'

She broke off again, dipping her head, shutting her eyes.

Weariness pressed in on him. 'Jenna, go back to England. Go back and be thankful…' Something twisted in his voice—he could not stop it. 'Be thankful you are done with me. For your lucky escape.'

Her eyes flared open, her head lifting. 'Escape?'

There was something in her voice that had not been there before. What it was he didn't know, but it did not stop him saying what he must say now. Roughly. Brusquely.

'Yes—escape! Go, Jenna. Flee as fast as you can.'

He wanted her to go. He couldn't take this any longer. Couldn't endure seeing her standing there— so close and yet so infinitely far away.

But she was not moving. She was standing stock-still, and what it was that had filled her voice was now filling her face…

He saw her think for a moment before speaking again. There was still that difference in her voice that he could not make out. And something different in the way she was looking at him as well. Something he could not comprehend. Her gaze clung to him, the intensity of it piercing.

'Evandro, that day—that day you sent me away. Tell me one thing and one thing only…'

There was hesitation in her voice now, and again he could not make out why. He saw her take a breath, as if steeling herself, then she spoke again, her voice low, intense. Insistent.

'If Berenice had never threatened to reclaim

Amelie would you have sent me away? Oh, perhaps not then, and not in the way you did, but when she started school…? Would you ever have sent me away?'

Her eyes, so clear, like spring water, were set on him. He could not escape them. Nor escape answering her.

A single word. All that he could say. All that was in him to say.

'No,' he said.

Jenna shut her eyes again. Weak with what she had done. Weak with the tumult of emotion pouring through her. So weak she could scarcely lift her eyelids to look at him again.

He had not moved, still standing by the open doorway, the sunlight still etching the dreadful scars across one side of his face.

But courage filled her, summoned into being by that single word he'd said. Courage and so much more.

All the love I have for him.

'So why,' she said, 'are you sending me away again?'

A savage look flashed across his ravaged face. 'Do you really think I would do anything else now?' he answered, his voice as low and savage as that look.

She filled her gaze with that same intensity and pinioned him. 'Now what?' she asked. Challenging him. 'Now that you have a limp and there are scars across your face?'

She walked towards him. He could send her away now and she would go—but for one reason and one only. The only reason that had any power at all.

Because he does not love me the way I love him. That is the only reason I would leave him now.

Emotion fuelled her.

She went on walking towards where he stood, dark against the sunlight beyond, tension in every line of his body.

'Don't do this, Jenna,' he said, his voice low. 'Don't waste yourself on me.'

She ignored him, halting a metre away from him. Never taking her eyes from him. She had something to say and he *would* hear her.

'Evandro, I will tell you this and you will hear me.' She made her voice clear—incontestable—as she said the words he had to hear. 'Of all that I know about you, I know this most of all: you show your love by protecting those you love—even at the cost of your own happiness. You showed it for Amelie, for the daughter you love so much—*your* daughter—by protecting her from Berenice, whatever it took. You protected me by sending me away, as harshly as you could, because you thought it would set me free to hate you. And now,' she said, and this was the final, most vital thing she had to say to him, 'you think this is another gift, don't you, Evandro? Freeing me from a man who thinks of himself as a "maimed and crippled wreck."'

She quoted his own cruel description of himself back at him and her expression changed as she put her final, vital question to him. The question on which depended all the happiness of her life.

'Do you really think, Evandro, that scars and a limp would stop me loving you?'

She heard her words resonate, heard the declaration that she could not, *would* not recall.

'I fell in love with you, Evandro. I fell in love with you and I will stay in love with you for ever. And not one of the scars on your face, or anywhere else, for that matter, can make a jot of difference!'

She took his hand, feeling the damaged scar tissue against her fingers, and looked up at him. She could see nothing in his face, but that did not matter now. She had to make him understand. Had to declare it all. Dare all.

'I love you, Evandro. And I don't know whether you love me back or not, but right now all I know is this. *This!*'

He was still looking at her with an expression she could not read, as she softly, clearly, spoke words written so long ago that still rang true.

'"Love is not love which alters when it alteration finds... O no! It is an ever-fixed mark that looks on tempests and is never shaken..."'

She gazed up at him, pouring her heart into her words, her gaze and her hands on his.

'*Never*, Evandro.' She spoke with absolute certainty. 'Hear that word. Understand it. *Never.*'

She let his hand fall away from her. In her chest she could feel her heart beating fast as she waited for his reply.

'Send me away or not, Evandro,' she said quietly, resolutely. 'It will *never* stop me loving you.'

He met her eyes. Melded his gaze with hers. For one long, endless moment he did not speak. And then…

'What have I done,' he said finally, his voice low and slow, 'to deserve you?'

He took back her hands, both of them, cradling them in his, and she could feel the welts on them where burning shards had scorched his flesh as he'd tried to rescue the woman who had wrought such terrible destruction. The look on his face stopped the breath in her.

'From the very first you have been a gift past all deserving—'

He broke off. Then spoke again, his voice still low, but filled now with an intensity of emotion that reached into the deepest recesses of her heart.

'Pushing you away like that was more pain than I ever want to feel again. And last night…' his face shadowed, etched with remembered darkness '…last night as I sat here, in my wrecked body, my wrecked home, knowing I could never ask…beg…you to come back to me, maimed as I am, I cried out to heaven with my desolation. I believed that Berenice's vengeance had been more thorough than she could ever have dreamt of—'

She freed a hand, laying a finger on his lips, silencing him. Berenice had been denied her victory.

'She's gone, Evandro. She's gone. For ever. She can hurt and damage and harm none of us any more.

And we have each other...' Joy was filling her, radiating outwards to embrace him, to embrace the whole world. *'For ever.'*

She let her fingers trace the ragged seams of his scars. Lifted her mouth to graze his softly, sweetly. Then drew back. In his eyes was all she had longed so much to see. All his love for her.

'My lovely, loving woodland sprite,' he said, his voice low and husky, 'whom I love so very much...'

Emotion was rich in his voice, and Jenna's overflowing heart swelled with radiant joy as she heard it.

He kissed her again, more deeply this time, and she felt tears dew on her lashes. But she would not shed them. This was not a time for tears...only for joy. Nothing but joy after so much heartache, and heartbreak, and tragedy, and pain. Now only joy—

For us both...for ever!

And for one more.

Footsteps sounded on the terrace, light and rapid.

'Papà! I'm home—are you in here?'

Amelie burst in through the open French doors, then halted dead in her tracks, dropping her school bag on the floor. Evandro lifted his mouth from Jenna's, but she felt his hand squeeze hers, not relinquishing it.

A cry of disbelieving delight and excitement broke from Amelie. 'You came! You came, you came, you came!'

She hurled herself at Jenna, and Jenna dropped down to hug her back, crushing Amelie to her, her heart overflowing all over again at seeing the little girl she had come to love so dearly.

'I wished and wished and prayed and prayed!' Amelie cried into Jenna's neck. 'And you came—you came!'

Jenna felt Evandro haltingly hunker down beside them. When he spoke his voice was warm and rich with love—for *both* of them, Jenna knew with another rush of joy.

'Yes, *carina*, she came—and we will never let her go again, will we?' His arm came around them, warm on Jenna's shoulder. 'Never.'

Her heart was singing and she was radiant with joy, rapturous with it. With a whole heavenly chorus of everlasting joy.

He straightened, and Jenna did likewise. She could see him wince at the pressure the movement put on his damaged leg.

'Poppet, your *papà* needs to sit down...'

Making a fuss of him, Amelie and Jenna helped Evandro to his leather armchair.

Evandro dropped a kiss on Amelie's head. '*Mignonne*, run and find Signora Farrafacci. Ask her for a bottle of champagne. For we are going to celebrate—now and for always! And do not hurry back *too* fast, because you see...' He bent his head and whispered something in a conspiratorial fashion to Amelie, whose face lit up before she hared off.

Evandro caught at Jenna's hand as she stood beside his chair. His slate-dark eyes glinted with gold and she felt her heart turn over, that heavenly chorus of joy inside her reaching a crescendo.

'I know that I should go down on one knee to say this,' he said, and there was a ruefulness in his voice as he spoke, 'but I might never be able to get back up again if I do, so instead—'

He drew her down to perch on the arm of the chair, taking her other hand as well, raising each to his lips in turn. His gaze was alight, pouring into hers, rich and lambent and full of love—oh, so full of love. And his voice, as he spoke, was deep and filled with all that she could ever want to hear.

'Will you, my beloved Jenna, be my own true love, all my life, and take my love for you all your life? You are my blessing and my joy, my heart's delight and my body's pleasure, the companion of my days…the passion of my nights. Be mine, as I am yours, for now and all eternity.'

She felt tears dew on her eyelashes again, and he kissed them away with soft kisses.

'Is that a yes?' he asked.

She could hear the humour in his voice—and so much more. A world of more…

'For now and all eternity,' she answered.

For one long, endless moment they gazed deep into each other's eyes, secure in the knowledge that all that had parted them had gone for ever. Then his mouth claimed hers again. She was his own true love—as she knew she always would be—and her heart soared higher yet with joy, and higher still.

Time stopped and eternity began—love's creation and its gift.

And then, as their endless kiss sealed their love, their happiness, the library doors were flung open and Amelie burst in again, followed by Signora Farrafacci bearing champagne, and Loretta and Maria holding champagne flutes and a jug of orange juice for Amelie.

There was a cacophony of congratulations and laughter and excitement and happiness, and Amelie dancing around in joyful glee, and the pop of the champagne cork, and the fetching of more glasses for the housekeeper and the maids as well, and the brimming of flutes... And Jenna was embracing everyone, and glasses were raised in toasts and salutations and felicitations such that the noise must reach heaven itself.

Except that heaven was surely here right now... and always would be.

Jenna's joy-filled eyes swept the happy throng before coming back, as they always would, to her beloved Evandro...

Mine, oh, mine at last. As I am his.

And would be—always and for ever now.

EPILOGUE

Amelie was messaging her friend.

Luisa, she's married him! I knew she would—I wished and wished, and prayed and prayed, and now she has! And I was bridesmaid. I wore a cream dress with lace on it and I will send you a photo, because it is lovely and I will keep it to wear again at special parties, my new mamma says.

It wasn't a big wedding, because poor Papà's bad leg is still not completely healed, and he has to have an operation on his eye so he can see properly again, and our home is still being repaired. It's very sad with it so much burnt down, and even sadder that my poor maman died, but Papà says she had a kind of illness inside her head, which is why I came to live here in Italy. I put flowers on her grave and the nuns pray for her, and so do I.

Reverend Mother says she is in heaven now, so she is not ill any more, or dead, because no one is ill or dead in heaven. And Reverend Mother says God has sent me a new mamma—not to take her place, but to be an extra mamma, one that's alive, and I can love her as well as Papà, which I do already.

And Papà asked would I like a baby brother or sister, like you already have, and I said yes, please, so he is going to ask Mamma to grow one especially for me. And for them, too, as they would love to have a baby as well, my new mamma says. And I can help choose names when he or she is born.

It will take quite a long time for the baby to grow, so we shall have Christmas by ourselves, and then we shall go to Sorrento for New Year, and they will have fireworks at sea, and I can watch them from the balcony of my great-aunt's house. She is very old, but I like her, and she is looking after the dolls' house Papà bought me in the summer from Naples.

I am going to stop now, because my fingers are tired and it is time for dinner. I can wear whatever outfit I like, Mamma says, because it is the weekend, so I am going to wear the frou-frou skirt with the sequinned top which I love, even though Mamma doesn't, but she doesn't say so, and nor does Papà, but he doesn't say so either. But my maman in heaven bought it for me, so I think I should wear it for her.

She said as much to Jenna when she came downstairs, and Jenna kissed her gently and said that it was the right thing to do. It had been hard for Amelie to learn that Berenice was dead, but at least she knew that her father had nearly died himself, trying to save her.

'I did try, *mignonne*. I promise you with all my

heart's love that I tried to save her,' he'd said, sad for the waste and tragedy of it all.

But Jenna's words echoed in him, helping him make what peace he could with Berenice's memory.

'No child is born bad. That's the first lesson a teacher must learn. Just as something made my father cold and unloving towards me, so something warped and twisted Berenice, even if we can't understand what it was. Maybe all we can say is that there was a sickness inside her—and we can understand her better for that, Evandro. Feel compassion because she was never able to know happiness, as we are blessed enough to know it.'

Her eyes went to Amelie, lighting with the love she felt for the little girl.

'And she gave us both so great a gift, Evandro,' she said quietly. 'She gave us your daughter. For Amelie *is* your daughter, by every measure that counts.'

'And yours,' he said, taking her into his arms. 'Never, for an instant, think otherwise.'

'Ours.' She smiled.

And as they went into dinner, hand in hand, Jenna remembered how they'd stood, the three of them, out on the terrace at sunset, and how she'd longed so much for what they now—thankfully, truly—were.

Family.

Loving and united.

For all their days.

* * * * *

Caught up in the magic of
Cinderella in the Boss's Palazzo?
You're sure to love these other stories
by Julia James!

Heiress's Pregnancy Scandal
Billionaire's Mediterranean Proposal
Irresistible Bargain with the Greek
The Greek's Duty-Bound Royal Bride
The Greek's Penniless Cinderella

All available now!

WE HOPE YOU ENJOYED
THIS BOOK FROM

⬡ HARLEQUIN

PRESENTS

Escape to exotic locations where passion knows no bounds.

Welcome to the glamorous lives of royals and billionaires,
where passion knows no bounds. Be swept into a world
of luxury, wealth and exotic locations.

8 NEW BOOKS AVAILABLE EVERY MONTH!

HPHALO2021

COMING NEXT MONTH FROM

⊞ HARLEQUIN
PRESENTS

Available April 27, 2021

#3905 PREGNANT WITH HIS MAJESTY'S HEIR
by Annie West
One reckless night with an unforgettable stranger leaves Aurélie expecting! She's scandalized to discover her baby's father is new king Lucien! Now she must confess all to the reluctant royal and await His Majesty's reaction...

#3906 THE RING THE SPANIARD GAVE HER
by Lynne Graham
Accepting billionaire Ruy's convenient proposal rescues innocent Suzy from a disastrous marriage...and creates a major problem: their raging chemistry! He's all icy control to her impulsive emotion. Soon returning his temporary ring feels like the biggest challenge of all...

#3907 CINDERELLA'S NIGHT IN VENICE
Signed, Sealed...Seduced
by Clare Connelly
When Ares insists shy Bea accompany him to a gala, she wants to refuse. The gorgeous Greek is as arrogant as he is charming, yet she can't say no to her PR firm's biggest client...or to one magical night in Venice!

#3908 HER DEAL WITH THE GREEK DEVIL
Rich, Ruthless & Greek
by Caitlin Crews
Virgin Molly knows the danger of walking into a powerful man's den. Yet only an outrageous deal with Greek billionaire Constantine will save her beloved mother. He has always been sinfully seductive but, bound by their pact, Molly burns for him. And there's no going back...

HPCNMRA0421

#3909 THE FORBIDDEN INNOCENT'S BODYGUARD
Billion-Dollar Mediterranean Brides
by Michelle Smart
Elsa's always been off-limits to self-made billionaire Santi. Now as her temporary bodyguard he'll offer her every luxury and every protection. To offer any more would be the most dangerous—yet tempting—mistake!

#3910 HOW TO WIN THE WILD BILLIONAIRE
South Africa's Scandalous Billionaires
by Joss Wood
Bay needs the job of revamping Digby's luxurious Cape Town hotel to win custody of her orphaned niece. That means resisting their off-the-charts chemistry, which is made harder when Digby gives her control over if—and when—she'll give in to his oh-so-tempting advances...

#3911 STRANDED FOR ONE SCANDALOUS WEEK
Rebels, Brothers, Billionaires
by Natalie Anderson
When playboy Ash arrives at his New Zealand island mansion, he never expects to encounter innocent Merle and their red-hot attraction. He's back for one week to lay his past to rest. Might he find solace in Merle instead...?

#3912 PROMOTED TO THE ITALIAN'S FIANCÉE
Secrets of the Stowe Family
by Cathy Williams
Heartbroken Izzy flees to California to reconnect with her past and finds herself in a business standoff with devastatingly handsome tycoon Gabriel. He's ready to bargain—if she first becomes nanny to his daughter...then his fake fiancée?

YOU CAN FIND MORE INFORMATION ON UPCOMING HARLEQUIN TITLES, FREE EXCERPTS AND MORE AT HARLEQUIN.COM.

HPCNMRB0421

SPECIAL EXCERPT FROM

⟨H⟩ HARLEQUIN

PRESENTS

*When Ares insists shy Bea accompany him to a gala,
she wants to refuse. The gorgeous Greek is as arrogant
as he is charming, yet she can't say no to her PR firm's
biggest client...or to one magical night in Venice!*

*Read on for a sneak preview of
Clare Connelly's next story for Harlequin Presents,*
Cinderella's Night in Venice.

As the car slowed to go over a speed bump, his fingers
briefly fell to her shoulder. An accident of transit, nothing
intentional about it. The reason didn't matter, though; the
spark of electricity was the same regardless. She gasped and
quickly turned her face away, looking beyond the window.

It was then that she realized they had driven through the
gates of City Airport.

Bea turned back to face Ares, a question in her eyes.

"There's a ball at the airport?"

"No."

"Then why...?" Comprehension was a blinding light.
"We're flying somewhere."

"To the ball."

"But...you didn't say..."

"I thought you were good at reading between the lines?"

She pouted her lips. "Yes, you're right." She clicked her
fingers in the air. "I should have miraculously intuited that
when you invited me to a ball you meant for us to fly there.
Where, exactly?"

"Venice."

"Venice?" She stared at him, aghast. "I don't have a
passport."

"I had your assistant arrange it."

"You—what? When?"

"When I left this morning."

"My assistant just handed over my passport?"

"You have a problem with that?"

"Well, gee, let me think about that a moment," she said, tapping a finger to the side of her lip. "You're a man I'd never set eyes on until yesterday and now you have in your possession a document that's of reasonably significant personal importance. You could say I find that a little invasive, yes."

He dropped his hand from the back of the seat, inadvertently brushing her arm as he moved, then lifted a familiar burgundy document from his pocket. "Now you have it in your possession. It was no conspiracy to kidnap you, Beatrice, simply a means to an end."

Clutching the passport in her hand, she stared down at it. No longer bothered by the fact he'd managed to convince her assistant to commandeer a document of such personal importance from her top drawer, she was knocked off-kilter by his use of her full name. Nobody called her Beatrice anymore. She'd been Bea for as long as she could remember. But her full name on his lips momentarily shoved the air from her lungs.

"Why didn't you just tell me?"

He lifted his shoulders. "I thought you might say no."

It was an important clue as to how he operated. This was a man who would do what he needed to achieve whatever he wanted. He'd chosen to invite her to this event, and so he'd done what he deemed necessary to have her there.

Don't miss
Cinderella's Night in Venice,
available May 2021 wherever
Harlequin Presents books and ebooks are sold.

Harlequin.com

Copyright © 2021 by Harlequin Books S.A.

HPEXP0421

Get 4 FREE REWARDS!

We'll send you 2 FREE Books plus 2 FREE Mystery Gifts.

Harlequin Presents books feature the glamorous lives of royals and billionaires in a world of exotic locations, where passion knows no bounds.

FREE Value Over $20

YES! Please send me 2 FREE Harlequin Presents novels and my 2 FREE gifts (gifts are worth about $10 retail). After receiving them, if I don't wish to receive any more books, I can return the shipping statement marked "cancel." If I don't cancel, I will receive 6 brand-new novels every month and be billed just $4.55 each for the regular-print edition or $5.80 each for the larger-print edition in the U.S., or $5.49 each for the regular-print edition or $5.99 each for the larger-print edition in Canada. That's a savings of at least 11% off the cover price! It's quite a bargain! Shipping and handling is just 50¢ per book in the U.S. and $1.25 per book in Canada.* I understand that accepting the 2 free books and gifts places me under no obligation to buy anything. I can always return a shipment and cancel at any time. The free books and gifts are mine to keep no matter what I decide.

Choose one: ☐ **Harlequin Presents Regular-Print** (106/306 HDN GNWY)   ☐ **Harlequin Presents Larger-Print** (176/376 HDN GNWY)

Name (please print)

Address   Apt. #

City   State/Province   Zip/Postal Code

Email: Please check this box ☐ if you would like to receive newsletters and promotional emails from Harlequin Enterprises ULC and its affiliates. You can unsubscribe anytime.

Mail to the **Harlequin Reader Service:**
IN U.S.A.: P.O. Box 1341, Buffalo, NY 14240-8531
IN CANADA: P.O. Box 603, Fort Erie, Ontario L2A 5X3

Want to try 2 free books from another series! Call 1-800-873-8635 or visit www.ReaderService.com.

---

*Terms and prices subject to change without notice. Prices do not include sales taxes, which will be charged (if applicable) based on your state or country of residence. Canadian residents will be charged applicable taxes. Offer not valid in Quebec. This offer is limited to one order per household. Books received may not be as shown. Not valid for current subscribers to Harlequin Presents books. All orders subject to approval. Credit or debit balances in a customer's account(s) may be offset by any other outstanding balance owed by or to the customer. Please allow 4 to 6 weeks for delivery. Offer available while quantities last.

Your Privacy—Your information is being collected by Harlequin Enterprises ULC, operating as Harlequin Reader Service. For a complete summary of the information we collect, how we use this information and to whom it is disclosed, please visit our privacy notice located at corporate.harlequin.com/privacy-notice. From time to time we may also exchange your personal information with reputable third parties. If you wish to opt out of this sharing of your personal information, please visit readerservice.com/consumerschoice or call 1-800-873-8635. **Notice to California Residents**—Under California law, you have specific rights to control and access your data. For more information on these rights and how to exercise them, visit corporate.harlequin.com/california-privacy.

HP21R